'Le Guin writes with painstaking intelligence. Her characters are complex and haunting, and her writing is remarkable for its sinewy grace' *Time*

'Le Guin is a writer of phenomenal power. She sets up enormous challenges and meets them fully; she invites, as Tolkien does, total belief' *Observer*

'I read her nonstop growing up and read her still'
Junot Diaz, Pulitzer Prize-winning author

Also by Ursula K. Le Guin

SF MASTERWORKS

The Word for World is Forest

URSULA K. Le GUIN

Text copyright © Ursula K. Le Guin 1972, 1976
Introduction copyright © Ken MacLeod 2014
All rights reserved

The right of Ursula K. Le Guin to be identified as the author
of this work, and the right of Ken MacLeod to be identified as
the author of the introduction, has been asserted by them in
accordance with the Copyright, Designs and Patents Act 1988.

This edition first published in Great Britain in 2015 by Gollancz
An imprint of the Orion Publishing Group
Orion House, 5 Upper St Martin's Lane,
London WC2H 9EA
An Hachette UK Company

7 9 10 8 6

A CIP catalogue record for this book
is available from the British Library

ISBN 978 1 473 20578 9

Printed and bound in Great Britain by Clays Ltd, Elcograf S.p.A.

The Orion Publishing Group's policy is to use papers
that are natural, renewable and recyclable products and
made from wood grown in sustainable forests. The logging
and manufacturing processes are expected to conform to
the environmental regulations of the country of origin.

www.orionbooks.co.uk
www.gollancz.co.uk

INTRODUCTION

Written in the glare of the United States' war on Indochina, and first published as a separate book in that war's dire aftermath, *The Word for World is Forest* is a reflection on invasion, exploitation and oppression, and on the necessity and cost of resistance.

Though short, the novel is far from slight. It brings into sharp focus several of its author's enduring concerns, and draws on the same intellectual resources that illuminate her wider work: notably anthropology, anarchism, feminism and Taoism. Characteristically of all Le Guin's writing, it embodies the stubborn virtue of seeing with both eyes, in depth and in colour, without looking away from or ignoring uncomfortable truths.

At the time of the novel's setting, some centuries in the future, Vietnam is history – a history well remembered by one of the characters, Colonel Dongh. The prevailing social system on Earth and its colonies is still some sort of state capitalism, by now the driver of an interstellar imperialism. Racism has mutated and evolved to the point where having recent African ancestry – rather than having no trace of it – is to the racist eye what makes one fully human. That venomous notion has been given its own cosmic inflation by the discovery that there are in reality more races than even the Victorians suspected: *Homo sapiens* has a common ancestry with a forerunner species, the still extant and annoyingly wise Hainish, who in the distant past settled many worlds, including Earth.

Also of Hainish (and of terrestrial) descent are the natives of Athshe, the world for which the word is forest. Gentle, tribal, matriarchal, and small, they are easy prey. Just strong enough to be slaves, too weak to be a threat, their likely fate is extinction. The forests in which they live are being felled around them to

clear ground for future settlement and to satisfy an insatiable
yearning for wood, a luxury almost beyond price back on the
deforested home planet.

If we read the tale at too literal a level, as some critics have
done, this makes no economic sense. It is almost inconceivable
that interstellar extractive exploitation across all those decades
of light-years could be profitable. Such nit-picking can sensibly
and safely be ignored. In the first place, we have no textual
evidence that it's even meant to make economic sense. Perhaps
it's a mere whim of businessmen-bureaucrats who have no need
to profit on their very long-term investment. Furthermore, in a
world where the kauri trees of New Zealand were felled and
sawn up to make (among other such vital necessities) decking
for yachts, and where the elephant is being driven close to
extinction for ivory trinkets, and the rhinoceros for the entirely
bogus medical virtues of powder made from its horn, and so on
(and on) and where Vietnam is still suffering grievously from the
effects of the chemical defoliants dumped on it at the very time
this book was being written . . . in such a world, one would think,
a writer crafting a protest is surely permitted some small poetic
license.

In the other great SF work to come out of what in Vietnam
is known as the American War, Joe Haldeman's *The Forever
War*, the conflict is between equally powerful empires and is in
the end revealed to be the result of mutual misunderstanding.
No such reassurance rounds off *The Word for World is Forest*.
The author's sympathy is entirely with the enemy. The invaders
from Earth are indisputably the bad guys and the rebellious
natives are entirely in the right. But the novel's revolutionary
defeatism doesn't fall into the trap of romanticising the revolt
of the oppressed. The Athsheans are changed by the very act of
fighting, new and strange to them; the world they win back is not
the same as the world that was taken from them; and their fight
is not fair, or discriminating, or by the rules. It is dirty and brutal
and shocking.

That oppression corrupts the oppressors is well enough
known. That resistance to oppression can profoundly change

those resisting, and for the worse, is less widely recognised – particularly among those who give that resistance their sympathy and solidarity. The ennobling aspect of resistance – of standing up, of fighting back, of driving the invader from the homeland – is seen and celebrated. The corrupting aspect – the hardening of the heart, the acceptance of casualty and atrocity, the replacement of the moral calculus with a cold-eyed calculation of advantage, of revenge and reprisal – is put out of mind, and sometimes for what seem the best of reasons. That too is part of the damage done.

Le Guin's subtle Taoist dialectic of darkness and light does not stop there. The Athsheans' world, we see and are told early on, is itself a failed and lost Hainish colony. Not only the hominids, but most or all of the planet's species of plants and animals are descended from a biota transplanted from Earth a million years ago. In showing us as an alien jungle and as a benign environment what is after all a forest such as might have covered Europe and North America in the Pleistocene, the novel gives its readers from those continents some further cause for reflection. And in implying that the now wise and compassionate Hainish were themselves invaders and colonisers in the distant past, this tale of damage and destruction carries a small, secret seed of hope for a better future than it depicts.

Ursula Le Guin may be the SF writer most respected by the literary mainstream, the most studied academically, her work set texts in countless courses. She remains subversive, and her work dangerous reading, because it changes the reader and makes them look at the real world in a different light. This novel's continuing relevance is a rebuke to our complacency.

Ken MacLeod

AUTHOR'S INTRODUCTION

1. *On What the Road to Hell is Paved With*

There is nothing in all Freud's writings that I like better than his assertion that artists' work is motivated by the desire "to achieve honour, power, riches, fame, and the love of women". It is such a comforting, such a complete statement; it explains everything about the artist. There have even been artists who agreed with it; Ernest Hemingway, for instance; at least, he said he wrote for money, and since he was an honoured, powerful, rich, famous artist beloved by women, he ought to know.

There is another statement about the artist's desires that is, to me, less obscure; the first two stanzas of it read,

> Riches I hold in light esteem
> And Love I laugh to scorn
> And lust of Fame was but a dream
> That vanished with the morn—
>
> And if I pray, the only prayer
> That moves my lips for me
> Is—"Leave the heart that now I bear
> And give me liberty."

Emily Brontë wrote those lines when she was twenty-two. She was a young and inexperienced woman, not honoured, not rich, not powerful, not famous, and you see that she was positively rude about love ("of women" or otherwise). I believe, however, that she was rather better qualified than Freud to talk about what motivates the artist. He had a theory. But she had authority.

It may well be useless, if not pernicious, to seek a single

motive for a pursuit so complex, long-pursued, and various as art; I imagine that Brontë got as close to it as anyone needs to get, with her word "liberty".

The pursuit of art, then, by artist or audience, is the pursuit of liberty. If you accept that, you see at once why truly serious people reject and mistrust the arts, labelling them as "escapism". The captured soldier tunnelling out of prison, the runaway slave, and Solzhenitsyn in exile, are escapists. Aren't they? The definition also helps explain why all healthy children can sing, dance, paint, and play with words; why art is an increasingly important element in psychotherapy; why Winston Churchill painted, why mothers sing cradle-songs, and what is wrong with Plato's *Republic*. It really is a much more useful statement than Freud's, though nowhere near as funny.

I am not sure what Freud meant by "power", in this context. Perhaps significantly, Brontë does not mention power. Shelley does, indirectly: "Poets are the unacknowledged legislators of the world. . . ." This is perhaps not too far from what Freud had in mind, for I doubt he was thinking of the artist's immediate and joyous power over his material—the shaping hand, the dancer's leap, the novelist's power of life and death over his characters; it is more probable that he meant the power of the idea to influence other people.

The desire for power, in the sense of power over others, is what pulls most people off the path of the pursuit of liberty. The reason Brontë does not mention it is probably that it was never even a temptation to her, as it was to her sister Charlotte. Emily did not give a damn about other people's morals. But many artists, particularly artists of the word, whose ideas must actually be spoken in their work, succumb to the temptation. They begin to see that they can do good to other people. They forget about liberty, then, and instead of legislating in divine arrogance, like God or Shelley, they begin to preach.

In this tale, *The Word for World is Forest*, which began as a pure pursuit of freedom and the dream, I succumbed, in part, to the lure of the pulpit. It is a very strong lure to a science fiction writer, who deals more directly than most novelists with ideas, whose metaphors are shaped by or embody ideas, and who therefore is always in danger of inextricably confusing ideas with opinions.

I wrote *The Little Green Men* (its first editor, Harlan Ellison, retitled it, with my rather morose permission) in the winter of 1968, during a year's stay in London. All through the sixties, in my home city in the States, I had been helping organise and participating in non-violent demonstrations, first against atomic bomb testing, then against the pursuance of the war in Viet Nam. I don't know how many times I walked down Alder Street in the rain, feeling useless, foolish, and obstinate, along with ten or twenty or a hundred other foolish and obstinate souls. There was always somebody taking pictures of us—not the press—odd-looking people with cheap cameras: John Birchers? FBI? CIA? Crackpots? No telling. I used to grin at them, or stick out my tongue. One of my fiercer friends brought a camera once and took pictures of the picture-takers. Anyhow, there was a peace movement, and I was in it, and so had a channel of action and expression for my ethical and political opinions totally separate from my writing.

In England that year, a guest and a foreigner, I had no such outlet. And 1968 was a bitter year for those who opposed the war. The lies and hypocrisies redoubled; so did the killing. Moreover, it was becoming clear that the ethic which approved the defoliation of forests and grainlands and the murder of non-combatants in the name of "peace" was only a corollary of the ethic which permits the despoliation of natural resources for private profit or the GNP, and the murder of the creatures of the Earth in the name of "man". The victory of the ethic of exploitation, in all societies, seemed as inevitable as it was disastrous.

It was from such pressures, internalised, that this story resulted: forced out, in a sense, against my conscious resistance. I have said elsewhere that I never wrote a story more easily, fluently, surely—and with less pleasure.

I knew, because of the compulsive quality of the composition, that it was likely to become a preachment, and I struggled against this. Say not the struggle naught availeth. Neither Lyubov nor Selver is mere Virtue Triumphant; moral and psychological complexity was salvaged, at least, in those characters. But Davidson is, though not uncomplex, pure; he is purely evil—and I don't, consciously, believe purely evil people exist. But my unconscious has other opinions. It looked into itself and produced, from itself, Captain Davidson. I do not disclaim him.

American involvement in Viet Nam is now past; the immediately intolerable pressures have shifted to other areas; and so the moralising aspects of the story are now plainly visible. These I regret, but I do not disclaim them either. The work must stand or fall on whatever elements it preserved of the yearning that underlies all specific outrage and protest, whatever tentative outreaching it made, amidst anger and despair, towards justice, or wit, or grace, or liberty.

2. *Synchronicity Can Happen*
At Almost Any Time

A few years ago, a few years after the first publication in America of *The Word for World is Forest*, I had the great pleasure of meeting Dr Charles Tart, a psychologist well known for his researches into and his book on *Altered States of Consciousness*. He asked me if I had modelled the Athsheans of the story upon the Senoi people of Malaysia. The who? said I, so he told me about them. The Senoi are, or were, a people whose culture includes and is indeed substantially based upon a deliberate training in and use of the dream. Dr Tart's book includes a brief article on them by Kilton Stewart.*

* "Dream Theory in Malaya", by Kilton Stewart, in *Altered States of Consciousness*, ed. Charles T. Tart, Wiley & Sons, 1969; Anchor-Doubleday, 1972. The quotations are on pp. 164 and 163 of the Anchor second edition.

Breakfast in the Senoi house is like a dream clinic, with the father and older brothers listening to and analysing the dreams of all the children. . . .

When the Senoi child reports a falling dream, the adult answers with enthusiasm, "That is a wonderful dream, one of the best dreams a man can have. Where did you fall to, and what did you discover?"

The Senoi dream is meaningful, active, and creative. Adults deliberately go into their dreams to solve problems of interpersonal and intercultural conflict. They come out of their dreams with a new song, tool, dance, idea. The waking and the dreaming states are equally valid, each acting upon the other in complementary fashion.

The article implies, by omission rather than by direct statement, that the men are the "great dreamers" among the Senoi; whether this means that the women are socially inferior, or that their role (as among the Athsheans) is equal and compensatory, is not clear. Nor is there any mention of the Senoi conception of divinity, the numinous, etc.; it is merely stated that they do not practise magic, though they are perfectly willing to let neighbouring peoples think they do, as this discourages invasion.

They have built a system of inter-personal relations which, in the field of psychology, is perhaps on a level with our attainments in such areas as television and nuclear physics.

It appears that the Senoi have not had a war, or a murder, for several hundred years.

There they are, twelve thousand of them, farming, hunting, fishing, and dreaming, in the rain forests of the mountains of Malaysia. Or there they were, in 1935—perhaps. Kilton Stewart's report on them has had no professional sequels that I know of. Were they ever there, and if so, are they still there? In the waking time, I mean, in what we so fantastically call "the real world". In the dream time, of course, they are there, and here. I thought I was inventing my own lot of imaginary aliens, and I was only describing the Senoi. It is not only the Captain Davidsons who can be found in the unconscious, if one looks. The quiet people who do not kill each other are there, too. It seems that a great deal is there, the things we most fear (and therefore deny), the things we most need (and therefore deny). I wonder, couldn't we start listening to our dreams, and our children's dreams?

"Where did you fall to, and what did you discover?"

Portland, 1976.

CHAPTER ONE

Two pieces of yesterday were in Captain Davidson's mind when he woke, and he lay looking at them in the darkness for a while. One up: the new shipload of women had arrived. Believe it or not. They were here, in Centralville, twenty-seven lightyears from Earth by NAFAL and four hours from Smith Camp by hopper, the second batch of breeding females for the New Tahiti Colony, all sound and clean, 212 head of prime human stock. Or prime enough, anyhow. One down: the report from Dump Island of crop failures, massive erosion, a wipe-out. The line of 212 buxom beddable breasty little figures faded from Davidson's mind as he saw rain pouring down onto ploughed dirt, churning it to mud, thinning the mud to a red broth that ran down rocks into the rain-beaten sea. The erosion had begun before he left Dump Island to run Smith Camp, and being gifted with an exceptional visual memory, the kind they called eidetic, he could recall it now all too clearly. It looked like that bigdome Kees was right and you had to leave a lot of trees standing where you planned to put farms. But he still couldn't see why a soybean farm needed to waste a lot of space on trees if the land was managed really scientifically. It wasn't like that in Ohio; if you wanted corn you grew corn, and no space wasted on trees and stuff. But then Earth was a tamed planet and New Tahiti wasn't. That's what he was here for: to tame it. If Dump Island was just rocks and gullies now, then scratch it; start over on a new island and do better. Can't keep us down, we're Men. You'll learn what that means pretty soon, you godforsaken damn planet, Davidson thought, and he grinned a little in the darkness of the hut, for he liked challenges. Thinking Men, he thought Women, and again the line of little figures began to sway through his mind, smiling, jiggling.

"Ben!" he roared, sitting up and swinging his bare feet onto the bare floor. "Hot water get-ready, hurry-up-quick!" The roar woke him satisfyingly. He stretched and scratched his chest and pulled on his shorts and strode out of the hut into the sunlit clearing all in one easy series of motions. A big, hard-muscled man, he enjoyed using his well-trained body. Ben, his creechie, had the water ready and steaming over the fire, as usual, and was squatting staring at nothing, as usual. Creechies never slept, they just sat and stared. "Breakfast. Hurry-up-quick!" Davidson said, picking up his razor from the rough board table where the creechie had laid it out ready with a towel and a propped-up mirror.

There was a lot to be done today, since he'd decided, that last minute before getting up, to fly down to Central and see the new women for himself. They wouldn't last long, 212 among over two thousand men, and like the first batch probably most of them were Colony Brides, and only twenty or thirty had come as Recreation Staff; but those babies were real good greedy girls and he intended to be first in line with at least one of them this time. He grinned on the left, the right cheek remaining stiff to the whining razor.

The old creechie was moseying round taking an hour to bring his breakfast from the cookhouse. "Hurry-up-quick!" Davidson yelled, and Ben pushed his boneless saunter into a walk. Ben was about a metre high and his back fur was more white than green; he was old, and dumb even for a creechie, but Davidson knew how to handle him. A lot of men couldn't handle creechies worth a damn, but Davidson had never had trouble with them; he could tame any of them, if it was worth the effort. It wasn't, though. Get enough humans here, build machines and robots, make farms and cities, and nobody would need the creechies any more. And a good thing too. For this world, New Tahiti, was literally made for men. Cleaned up and cleaned out, the dark forests cut down for

open fields of grain, the primeval murk and savagery and
ignorance wiped out, it would be a paradise, a real Eden.
A better world than worn-out Earth. And it would be his
world. For that's what Don Davidson was, way down deep
inside him: a world-tamer. He wasn't a boastful man, but he
knew his own size. It just happened to be the way he was
made. He knew what he wanted, and how to get it. And he
always got it.

Breakfast landed warm in his belly. His good mood wasn't
spoiled even by the sight of Kees Van Sten coming towards
him, fat, white, and worried, his eyes sticking out like blue
golf-balls.

"Don," Kees said without greeting, "the loggers have been
hunting red deer in the Strips again. There are eighteen pair
of antlers in the back room of the Lounge."

"Nobody ever stopped poachers from poaching, Kees."

"You can stop them. That's why we live under martial
law, that's why the Army runs this colony. To keep the
laws."

A frontal attack from Fatty Bigdome! It was almost
funny. "All right," Davidson said reasonably, "I could stop
'em. But look, it's the men I'm looking after; that's my job,
like you said. And it's the men that count. Not the animals.
If a little extra-legal hunting helps the men get through
this godforsaken life, then I intend to blink. They've got to
have some recreation."

"They have games, sports, hobbies, films, teletapes of every
major sporting event of the past century, liquor, marijuana,
hallies, and a fresh batch of women at Central. For those un-
satisfied by the Army's rather unimaginative arrangements
for hygienic homosexuality. They are spoiled rotten, your
frontier heroes, and they don't need to exterminate a rare
native species 'for recreation'. If you don't act, I must record
a major infraction of Ecological Protocols in my report to
Captain Gosse."

"You can do that if you see fit, Kees," said Davidson, who
never lost his temper. It was sort of pathetic the way a euro

like Kees got all red in the face when he lost control of his emotions. "That's your job, after all. I won't hold it against you; they can do the arguing at Central and decide who's right. See, you want to keep this place just like it is, actually, Kees. Like one big National Forest. To look at, to study. Great, you're a spesh. But see we're just ordinary joes getting the work done. Earth needs wood, needs it bad. We find wood on New Tahiti. So—we're loggers. See, where we differ is that with you Earth doesn't come first, actually. With me it does."

Kees looked at him sideways out of those blue golf-ball eyes. "Does it? You want to make this world into Earth's image, eh? A desert of cement?"

"When I say Earth, Kees, I mean people. Men. You worry about deer and trees and fibreweed, fine, that's your thing. But I like to see things in perspective, from the top down, and the top, so far, is humans. We're here, now; and so this world's going to go our way. Like it or not, it's a fact you have to face; it happens to be the way things are. Listen, Kees, I'm going to hop down to Central and take a look at the new colonists. Want to come along?"

"No thanks, Captain Davidson," the spesh said, going on towards the Lab hut. He was really mad. All upset about those damn deer. They were great animals, all right. Davidson's vivid memory recalled the first one he had seen, here on Smith Land, a big red shadow, two metres at the shoulder, a crown of narrow golden antlers, a fleet, brave beast, the finest game-animal imaginable. Back on Earth they were using robodeer even in the High Rockies and Himalaya Parks now, the real ones were about gone. These things were a hunter's dream. So they'd be hunted. Hell, even the wild creechies hunted them, with their lousy little bows. The deer would be hunted because that's what they were there for. But poor old bleeding-heart Kees couldn't see it. He was actually a smart fellow, but not realistic, not tough-minded enough. He didn't see that you've got to play on the winning side or else you lose. And it's Man that wins, every time. The old Conquistador.

Davidson strode on through the settlement, morning sunlight in his eyes, the smell of sawn wood and woodsmoke sweet on the warm air. Things looked pretty neat, for a logging camp. The two hundred men here had tamed a fair patch of wilderness in just three E-months. Smith Camp: a couple of big corruplast geodesics, forty timber huts built by creechie-labour, the sawmill, the burner trailing a blue plume over acres of logs and cut lumber; uphill, the airfield and the big prefab hangar for helicopters and heavy machinery. That was all. But when they came here there had been nothing. Trees. A dark huddle and jumble and tangle of trees, endless, meaningless. A sluggish river overhung and choked by trees, a few creechie-warrens hidden among the trees, some red deer, hairy monkeys, birds. And trees. Roots, boles, branches, twigs, leaves, leaves overhead and underfoot and in your face and in your eyes, endless leaves on endless trees.

New Tahiti was mostly water, warm shallow sea broken here and there by reefs, islets, archipelagoes, and the five big Lands that lay in a 2500-kilo arc across the Northwest Quartersphere. And all those flecks and blobs of land were covered with trees. Ocean: forest. That was your choice on New Tahiti. Water and sunlight, or darkness and leaves.

But men were here now to end the darkness, and turn the tree-jumble into clean sawn planks, more prized on Earth than gold. Literally, because gold could be got from seawater and from under the Antarctic ice, but wood could not; wood came only from trees. And it was a really necessary luxury on Earth. So the alien forests became wood. Two hundred men with robosaws and haulers had already cut eight mile-wide Strips on Smith Land, in three months. The stumps of the Strip nearest camp were already white and punky; chemically treated, they would have fallen into fertile ash by the time the permanent colonists, the farmers, came to settle Smith Land. All the farmers would have to do was plant seeds and let 'em sprout.

It had been done once before. That was a queer thing, and

the proof, actually, that New Tahiti was intended for humans to take over. All the stuff here had come from Earth, about a million years ago, and the evolution had followed so close a path that you recognised things at once: pine, oak, walnut, chestnut, fir, holly, apple, ash; deer, bird, mouse, cat, squirrel, monkey. The humanoids on Hain-Davenant of course claimed they'd done it at the same time as they colonised Earth, but if you listened to those ETs you'd find they claimed to have settled every planet in the Galaxy and invented everything from sex to thumbtacks. The theories about Atlantis were a lot more realistic, and this might well be a lost Atlantean colony. But the humans had died out. And the nearest thing that had developed from the monkey line to replace them was the creechie—a metre tall and covered with green fur. As ETs they were about standard, but as men they were a bust, they just hadn't made it. Give 'em another million years, maybe. But the Conquistadors had arrived first. Evolution moved now not at the pace of a random mutation once a millennium, but with the speed of the starships of the Terran Fleet.

"Hey Captain!"

Davidson turned, only a microsecond late in his reaction, but that was late enough to annoy him. There was something about this damn planet, its gold sunlight and hazy sky, its mild winds smelling of leafmould and pollen, something that made you daydream. You mooched along thinking about conquistadors and destiny and stuff, till you were acting as thick and slow as a creechie. "Morning, Ok!" he said crisply to the logging foreman.

Black and tough as wire rope, Oknanawi Nabo was Kees's physical opposite, but he had the same worried look. "You got half a minute?"

"Sure. What's eating you, Ok?"

"The little bastards."

They leaned their backsides on a split rail fence. Davidson lit his first reefer of the day. Sunlight, smoke-blued, slanted warm across the air. The forest behind camp, a quarter-mile-wide uncut strip, was full of the faint, ceaseless, cracking, chuckling, stirring, whirring, silvery noises that woods in the morning are full of. It might have been Idaho in 1950, this clearing. Or Kentucky in 1830. Or Gaul in 50 B.C. "Te-whet," said a distant bird.

"I'd like to get rid of 'em, Captain."

"The creechies? How d'you mean, Ok?"

"Just let 'em go. I can't get enough work out of 'em in the mill to make up for their keep. Or for their being such a damn headache. They just don't work."

"They do if you know how to make 'em. They built the camp."

Oknanawi's obsidian face was dour. "Well, you got the touch with 'em, I guess. I don't." He paused. "In that Applied History course I took in training for Far-out, it said that slavery never worked. It was uneconomical."

"Right, but this isn't slavery, Ok baby. Slaves are humans. When you raise cows, you call that slavery? No. And it works."

Impassive, the foreman nodded; but he said, "They're too little. I tried starving the sulky ones. They just sit and starve."

"They're little, all right, but don't let 'em fool you, Ok. They're tough; they've got terrific endurance; and they don't feel pain like humans. That's the part you forget, Ok. You think hitting one is like hitting a kid, sort of. Believe me, it's more like hitting a robot for all they feel it. Look, you've laid some of the females, you know how they don't seem to feel anything, no pleasure, no pain, they just lay there like mattresses no matter what you do. They're all like that. Probably they've got more primitive nerves than humans do. Like fish. I'll tell you a weird one about that. When I was in Central, before I came up here, one of the tame males jumped me once. I know they'll tell you they never fight, but this one went spla, right off his nut, and lucky he wasn't armed or he'd have killed me. I had to damn near kill him before he'd even let go. And he kept coming back. It was incredible the beating he took and never even felt it. Like some beetle you have to keep stepping on because it doesn't know it's been squashed already. Look at this." Davidson bent down his close-cropped head to show a gnarled lump behind one ear. "That was damn near a concussion. And he did it after I'd broken his arm and pounded his face into cranberry sauce. He just kept coming back and coming back. The thing is, Ok, the creechies are lazy, they're dumb, they're treacherous, and they don't feel pain. You've got to be tough with 'em, and stay tough with 'em."

"They aren't worth the trouble, Captain. Damn sulky little green bastards, they won't fight, won't work, won't nothing. Except give me the pip." There was a geniality in Oknanawi's grumbling which did not conceal the stubbornness beneath. He wouldn't beat up creechies because they were so much smaller; that was clear in his mind, and clear now to David-son, who at once accepted it. He knew how to handle his men. "Look, Ok. Try this. Pick out the ringleaders and tell 'em you're going to give them a shot of hallucinogen. Mesc, lice, any one, they don't know one from the other. But they're scared of them. Don't overwork it, and it'll work. I can guarantee."

"Why are they scared of hallies?" the foreman asked curiously.

"How do I know? Why are women scared of rats? Don't look for good sense from women or creechies, Ok! Speaking of which I'm on the way to Central this morning, shall I put the finger on a Collie Girl for you?"

"Just keep the finger off a few till I get my leave," Ok said grinning. A group of creechies passed, carrying a long 12 × 12 beam for the Rec Room being built down by the river. Slow, shambling little figures, they worried the big beam along like a lot of ants with a dead caterpillar, sullen and inept. Oknanawi watched them and said, "Fact is, Captain, they give me the creeps."

That was queer, coming from a tough, quiet guy like Ok.

"Well, I agree with you, actually, Ok, that they're not

worth the trouble, or the risk. If that fart Lyubov wasn't around and the Colonel wasn't so stuck on following the Code, I think we might just clean out the areas we settle, instead of this Voluntary Labour routine. They're going to get rubbed out sooner or later, and it might as well be sooner. It's just how things happen to be. Primitive races always have to give way to civilised ones. Or be assimilated. But we sure as hell can't assimilate a lot of green monkeys. And like you say, they're just bright enough that they'll never be quite trustworthy. Like those big monkeys used to live in Africa, what were they called."

"Gorillas?"

"Right. We'll get on better without creechies here, just like we get on better without gorillas in Africa. They're in our way. . . . But Daddy Ding-Dong he say use creechie-labour, so we use creechie-labour. For a while. Right? See you tonight, Ok."

"Right, Captain."

Davidson checked out the hopper from Smith Camp HQ: a pine-plank 4-metre cube, two desks, a watercooler, Lt. Birno repairing a walkytalky. "Don't let the camp burn down, Birno."

"Bring me back a Collie, Cap. Blonde. 34-22-36."

"Christ, is that all?"

"I like 'em neat, not floppy, see." Birno expressively outlined his preference in the air. Grinning, Davidson went on up to the hangar. As he brought the helicopter back over camp he looked down at it: kid's blocks, sketch-lines of paths, long stump-stubbled clearings, all shrinking as the machine rose and he saw the green of the uncut forests of the great island, and beyond that dark green the pale green of the sea going on and on. Now Smith Camp looked like a yellow spot, a fleck on a vast green tapestry.

He crossed Smith Straits and the wooded, deep-folded ranges of north Central Island, and came down by noon in Centralville. It looked like a city, at least after three months in the woods; there were real streets, real buildings, it had

been there since the Colony began four years ago. You didn't
see what a flimsy little frontier-town it really was, until
you looked south of it a halfmile and saw glittering above
the stumplands and the concrete pads a single golden tower,
taller than anything in Centralville. The ship wasn't a big
one but it looked so big, here. And it was only a launch, a
lander, a ship's boat; the NAFAL ship of the line, *Shackleton*,
was half a million kilos up, in orbit. The launch was just a
hint, just a fingertip of the hugeness, the power, the golden
precision and grandeur of the starbridging technology of
Earth.

That was why tears came to Davidson's eyes for a second
at the sight of the ship from home. He wasn't ashamed of it.
He was a patriotic man, it just happened to be the way he
was made.

Soon enough, walking down those frontier-town streets
with their wide vistas of nothing much at each end, he began
to smile. For the women were there, all right, and you could
tell they were fresh ones. They mostly had long tight skirts
and big shoes like goloshes, red or purple or gold, and gold
or silver frilly shirts. No more nipplepeeps. Fashions had
changed; too bad. They all wore their hair piled up high,
it must be sprayed with that glue stuff they used. Ugly as
hell, but it was the sort of thing only women would do to
their hair, and so it was provocative. Davidson grinned at a
chesty little euraf with more hair than head; he got no smile,
but a wag of the retreating hips that said plainly, Follow
follow follow me. But he didn't. Not yet. He went to Central
HQ: quickstone and plastiplate Standard Issue, 40 offices, 10
watercoolers and a basement arsenal, and checked in with
New Tahiti Central Colonial Administration Command. He
met a couple of the launch-crew, put in a request for a new
semirobo barkstripper at Forestry, and got his old pal Juju
Sereng to meet him at the Luau Bar at fourteen hundred.

He got to the bar an hour early to stock up on a little
food before the drinking began. Lyubov was there, sitting with
a couple of guys in Fleet uniform, some kind of speshes

that had come down on the *Shackleton*'s launch. Davidson didn't have a high regard for the Navy, a lot of fancy sun-hoppers who left the dirty, muddy, dangerous on-planet work to the Army; but brass was brass, and anyhow it was funny to see Lyubov acting chummy with anybody in uniform. He was talking, waving his hands around the way he did. Just in passing Davidson tapped his shoulder and said, "Hi, Raj old pal, how's tricks?" He went on without waiting for the scowl, though he hated to miss it. It was really funny the way Lyubov hated him. Probably the guy was effeminate like a lot of intellectuals, and resented Davidson's virility. Anyhow Davidson wasn't going to waste any time hating Lyubov, he wasn't worth the trouble.

The Luau served a first-rate venison steak. What would they say on old Earth if they saw one man eating a kilogram of meat at one meal? Poor damn soybeansuckers! Then Juju arrived with—as Davidson had confidently expected—the pick of the new Collie Girls: two fruity beauties, not Brides, but Recreation Staff. Oh the old Colonial Administration sometimes came through! It was a long, hot afternoon.

Flying back to camp he crossed Smith Straits level with the sun that lay on top of a great gold bed of haze over the sea. He sang as he lolled in the pilot's seat. Smith Land came in sight hazy, and there was smoke over the camp, a dark smudge as if oil had got into the waste-burner. He couldn't even make out the buildings through it. It was only as he dropped down to the landing-field that he saw the charred jet, the wrecked hoppers, the burned-out hangar.

He pulled the hopper up again and flew back over the camp, so low that he might have hit the high cone of the burner, the only thing left sticking up. The rest was gone, mill, furnace, lumberyards, HQ, huts, barracks, creechie compound, everything. Black hulks and wrecks, still smoking. But it hadn't been a forest fire. The forest stood there, green, next to the ruins. Davidson swung back round to the field, set down and lit out looking for the motorbike, but it too was a black wreck along with the stinking, smouldering ruins of the hangar and the machinery. He loped down the path to camp. As he passed what had been the radio hut, his mind snapped back into gear. Without hesitating for even a stride he changed course, off the path, behind the gutted shack. There he stopped. He listened.

There was nobody. It was all silent. The fires had been out a long time; only the great lumber-piles still smouldered, showing a hot red under the ash and char. Worth more than gold, those oblong ash-heaps had been. But no smoke rose from the black skeletons of the barracks and huts; and there were bones among the ashes.

Davidson's brain was super-clear and active, now, as he crouched behind the radio shack. There were two possibilities. One: an attack from another camp. Some officer on King or New Java had gone spla and was trying a coup de planète. Two: an attack from off-planet. He saw the golden tower on the space-dock at Central. But if the *Shackleton* had gone privateer why would she start by rubbing out a small camp, instead of taking over Centralville? No, it must be invasion, aliens. Some unknown race, or maybe the Cetians or the Hainish had decided to move in on Earth's colonies. He'd never trusted those damned smart humanoids. This must have been done with a heatbomb. The invading force, with jets, aircars, nukes, could easily be hidden on an island or reef anywhere in the SW Quartersphere. He must get back to his hopper and send out the alarm, then try a look around, reconnoitre, so he could tell HQ his assessment of the actual situation. He was just straightening up when he heard the voices.

Not human voices. High, soft, gabble-gobble. Aliens.

Ducking on hands and knees behind the shack's plastic roof, which lay on the ground deformed by heat into a bat-wing shape, he held still and listened.

Four creechies walked by a few yards from him, on the path. They were wild creechies, naked except for loose leather belts on which knives and pouches hung. None wore the shorts and leather collar supplied to tame creechies. The Volun-

teers in the compound must have been incinerated along with
the humans.

They stopped a little way past his hiding-place, talking their
slow gabble-gobble, and Davidson held his breath. He didn't
want them to spot him. What the devil were creechies doing
here? They could only be serving as spies and scouts for the
invaders.

One pointed south as it talked, and turned, so that
Davidson saw its face. And he recognised it. Creechies all
looked alike, but this one was different. He had written his
own signature all over that face, less than a year ago. It was
the one that had gone spla and attacked him down in Central,
the homicidal one, Lyubov's pet. What in the blue hell was
it doing here?

Davidson's mind raced, clicked; reactions fast as always, he
stood up, sudden, tall, easy, gun in hand. "You creechies.
Stop. Stay-put. No moving!"

His voice cracked out like a whiplash. The four little green
creatures did not move. The one with the smashed-in face
looked at him across the black rubble with huge, blank eyes
that had no light in them.

"Answer now. This fire, who start it?"

No answer.

"Answer now: hurry-up-quick! No answer, then I burn-up
first one, then one, then one, see? This fire, who start it?"

"We burned the camp, Captain Davidson," said the one
from Central, in a queer soft voice that reminded Davidson of
some human. "The humans are all dead."

"You burned it, what do you mean?"

He could not recall Scarface's name for some reason.

"There were two hundred humans here. Ninety slaves of
my people. Nine hundred of my people came out of the
forest. First we killed the humans in the place in the forest
where they were cutting trees, then we killed those in this
place, while the houses were burning. I had thought you
were killed. I am glad to see you, Captain Davidson."

It was all crazy, and of course a lie. They couldn't have

killed all of them, Ok, Birno, Van Sten, all the rest, two hundred men, some of them would have got out. All the creechies had was bows and arrows. Anyway the creechies couldn't have done this. Creechies didn't fight, didn't kill, didn't have wars. They were intraspecies non-aggressive, that meant sitting ducks. They didn't fight back. They sure as hell didn't massacre two hundred men at a swipe. It was crazy. The silence, the faint stink of burning in the long, warm evening light, the pale-green faces with unmoving eyes that watched him, it all added up to nothing, to a crazy bad dream, a nightmare.

"Who did this for you?"

"Nine hundred of my people," Scarface said in that damned fake-human voice.

"No, not that. Who else? Who were you acting for? Who told you what to do?"

"My wife did."

Davidson saw then the telltale tension of the creature's stance, yet it sprang at him so lithe and oblique that his shot missed, burning an arm or shoulder instead of smack between the eyes. And the creechie was on him, half his size and weight yet knocking him right off balance by its onslaught, for he had been relying on the gun and not expecting attack. The thing's arms were thin, tough, coarse-furred in his grip, and as he struggled with it, it sang.

He was down on his back, pinned down, disarmed. Four green muzzles looked down at him. The scarfaced one was still singing, a breathless gabble, but with a tune to it. The other three listened, their white teeth showing in grins. He had never seen a creechie smile. He had never looked up into a creechie's face from below. Always down, from above. From on top. He tried not to struggle, for at the moment it was wasted effort. Little as they were, they outnumbered him, and Scarface had his gun. He must wait. But there was a sickness in him, a nausea that made his body twitch and strain against his will. The small hands held him down effortlessly, the small green faces bobbed over him grinning.

Scarface ended his song. He knelt on Davidson's chest, a knife in one hand, Davidson's gun in the other.

"You can't sing, Captain Davidson, is that right? Well, then, you may run to your hopper, and fly away, and tell the Colonel in Central that this place is burned and the humans are all killed."

Blood, the same startling red as human blood, clotted the fur of the creechie's right arm, and the knife shook in the green paw. The sharp, scarred face looked down into Davidson's from very close, and he could see now the queer light that burned way down in the charcoal-dark eyes. The voice was still soft and quiet.

They let him go.

He got up cautiously, still dizzy from the fall Scarface had given him. The creechies stood well away from him now, knowing his reach was twice theirs; but Scarface wasn't the only one armed, there was a second gun pointing at his guts. That was Ben holding the gun. His own creechie Ben, the little grey mangy bastard, looking stupid as always but holding a gun.

It's hard to turn your back on two pointing guns, but Davidson did it and started walking towards the field.

A voice behind him said some creechie word, shrill and loud. Another said, "Hurry-up-quick!" and there was a queer noise like birds twittering that must be creechie laughter. A shot clapped and whined on the road right by him. Christ, it wasn't fair, they had the guns and he wasn't armed. He began to run. He could outrun any creechie. They didn't know how to shoot a gun.

"Run," said the quiet voice far behind him. That was Scarface—Selver, that was his name. Sam, they'd called him, till Lyubov stopped Davidson from giving him what he deserved and made a pet out of him, then they'd called him Selver. Christ, what was all this, it was a nightmare. He ran. The blood thundered in his ears. He ran through the golden, smoky evening. There was a body by the path, he hadn't even noticed it coming. It wasn't burned, it looked like a white balloon with the air gone out. It had staring blue eyes. They didn't dare kill him, Davidson. They hadn't shot at him again. It was impossible. They couldn't kill him. There was the hopper, safe and shining, and he lunged into the seat and had her up before the creechies could try anything. His hands shook, but not much, just shock. They couldn't kill him. He circled the hill and then came back fast and low, looking for the four creechies. But nothing moved in the streaky rubble of the camp.

There had been a camp there this morning. Two hundred men. There had been four creechies there just now. He hadn't dreamed all this. They couldn't just disappear. They were there, hiding. He opened up the machinegun in the hopper's nose and raked the burned ground, shot holes in the green leaves of the forest, strafed the burned bones and cold bodies of his men and the wrecked machinery and the rotting white stumps, returning again and again until the ammo was gone and the gun's spasms stopped short.

Davidson's hands were steady now, his body felt appeased, and he knew he wasn't caught in any dream. He headed back over the Straits, to take the news to Centralville. As he flew he could feel his face relax into its usual calm lines. They couldn't blame the disaster on him, for he hadn't even been there. Maybe they'd see that it was significant that the creechies had struck while he was gone, knowing they'd fail if he was there to organise the defence. And there was one good thing would come out of this. They'd do like they should have done to start with, and clean up the planet for human occupation. Not even Lyubov could stop them from rubbing out the creechies now, not when they heard it was Lyubov's pet creechie who'd led the massacre! They'd go in for rat-extermination for a while, now; and maybe, just maybe, they'd hand that little job over to him. At that thought he could have smiled. But he kept his face calm.

The sea under him was greyish with twilight, and ahead of him lay the island hills, the deep-folded, many-streamed, many-leaved forests in the dusk.

CHAPTER TWO

All the colours of rust and sunset, brown-reds and pale greens, changed ceaselessly in the long leaves as the wind blew. The roots of the copper willows, thick and ridged, were moss-green down by the running water, which like the wind moved slowly with many soft eddies and seeming pauses, held back by rocks, roots, hanging and fallen leaves. No way was clear, no light unbroken, in the forest. Into wind, water, sunlight, starlight, there always entered leaf and branch, bole and root, the shadowy, the complex. Little paths ran under the branches, around the boles, over the roots; they did not go straight, but yielded to every obstacle, devious as nerves. The ground was not dry and solid but damp and rather springy, product of the collaboration of living things with the long, elaborate death of leaves and trees; and from that rich graveyard grew ninety-foot trees, and tiny mushrooms that sprouted in circles half an inch across. The smell of the air was subtle, various, and sweet. The view was never long, unless looking up through the branches you caught sight of the stars. Nothing was pure, dry, arid, plain. Revelation was lacking. There was no seeing everything at once: no certainty. The colours of rust and sunset kept changing in the hanging leaves of the copper willows, and you could not say even whether the leaves of the willows were brownish-red, or reddish-green, or green.

Selver came up a path beside the water, going slowly and often stumbling on the willow roots. He saw an old man dreaming, and stopped. The old man looked at him through the long willow-leaves and saw him in his dreams.

"May I come to your Lodge, my Lord Dreamer? I've come a long way."

The old man sat still. Presently Selver squatted down on his heels just off the path, beside the stream. His head drooped down, for he was worn out and had to sleep. He had been walking for five days.

"Are you of the dream-time or of the world-time?" the old man asked at last.

"Of the world-time."

"Come along with me then." The old man got up promptly and led Selver up the wandering path out of the willow grove, into dryer, darker regions of oak and thorn. "I took you for a god," he said, going a pace ahead. "And it seemed to me I had seen you before, perhaps in dream."

"Not in the world-time. I come from Sornol, I have never been here before."

"This town is Cadast. I am Coro Mena. Of the Whitethorn."

"Selver is my name. Of the Ash."

"There are Ash people among us, both men and women. Also your marriage-clans, Birch and Holly; we have no women of the Apple. But you don't come looking for a wife, do you?"

"My wife is dead," Selver said.

They came to the Men's Lodge, on high ground in a stand of young oaks. They stooped and crawled through the tunnel-entrance. Inside, in the firelight, the old man stood up, but Selver stayed crouching on hands and knees, unable to rise. Now that help and comfort was at hand his body, which he had forced too far, would not go farther. It lay down and the eyes closed; and Selver slipped, with relief and gratitude, into the great darkness.

The men of the Lodge of Cadast looked after him, and their healer came to tend the wound in his right arm. In the night Coro Mena and the healer Torber sat by the fire. Most of the other men were with their wives that night; there were only a couple of young prentice-dreamers over on the benches, and they had both gone fast asleep. "I don't know what would give a man such scars as he has on his face," said the healer, "and much less, such a wound as that in his arm. A very queer wound."

"It's a queer engine he wore on his belt," said Coro Mena. "I saw it and didn't see it."

"I put it under his bench. It looks like polished iron, but not like the handiwork of men."

"He comes from Sornol, he said to you."

They were both silent awhile. Coro Mena felt unreasoning fear press upon him, and slipped into dream to find the reason for the fear; for he was an old man, and long adept. In the dream the giants walked, heavy and dire. Their dry scaly limbs were swathed in cloths; their eyes were little and light, like tin beads. Behind them crawled huge moving things made of polished iron. The trees fell down in front of them.

Out from among the falling trees a man ran, crying aloud, with blood on his mouth. The path he ran on was the door-path of the Lodge of Cadast.

"Well, there's little doubt of it," Coro Mena said, sliding out of the dream. "He came oversea straight from Sornol, or else came afoot from the coast of Kelme Deva on our own land. The giants are in both those places, travellers say."

"Will they follow him," said Torber; neither answered the question, which was no question but a statement of possibility.

"You saw the giants once, Coro?"

"Once," the old man said.

He dreamed; sometimes, being very old and not so strong as he had been, he slipped off to sleep for a while. Day broke, noon passed. Outside the Lodge a hunting-party went out, children chirped, women talked in voices like running water. A dryer voice called Coro Mena from the door. He crawled out into the evening sunlight. His sister stood outside, sniffing the aromatic wind with pleasure, but looking stern all the same. "Has the stranger waked up, Coro?"

"Not yet. Torber's looking after him."

"We must hear his story."

"No doubt he'll wake soon."

Ebor Dendep frowned. Headwoman of Cadast, she was anxious for her people; but she did not want to ask that a hurt man be disturbed, nor to offend the Dreamers by insisting on her right to enter their Lodge. "Can't you wake him, Coro?" she asked at last. "What if he is ... being pursued?"

He could not run his sister's emotions on the same rein with his own, yet he felt them; her anxiety bit him. "If Torber permits, I will," he said.

"Try to learn his news, quickly. I wish he was a woman and would talk sense. ..."

The stranger had roused himself, and lay feverish in the halfdark of the Lodge. The unreined dreams of illness moved in his eyes. He sat up, however, and spoke with control. As he listened Coro Mena's bones seemed to shrink within him trying to hide from this terrible story, this new thing.

"I was Selver Thele, when I lived in Eshreth in Sornol. My city was destroyed by the yumens when they cut down the trees in that region. I was one of those made to serve them, with my wife Thele. She was raped by one of them and died. I attacked the yumen that killed her. He would have killed me then, but another of them saved me and set me free. I left Sornol, where no town is safe from the yumens now, and came here to the North Isle, and lived on the coast of Kelme Deva in the Red Groves. There presently the yumens came and began to cut down the world. They destroyed a city there, Penle. They caught a hundred of the men and women and made them serve them, and live in the pen. I was not caught. I lived with others who had escaped from Penle, in the bogland north of Kelme Deva. Sometimes at night I went among the people in the yumen's pens. They told me that that one was there. That one whom I had tried to kill. I thought at first to try again; or else to set the people in the pen free. But all the time I watched the trees fall and saw the world cut open and left to rot. The men might have escaped, but the women were locked in more safely and could not, and they were beginning to die. I talked with the people hiding there in the boglands. We were all very frightened and very angry, and had no way to let our fear and anger free. So at last after long talking, and long dreaming, and the making of a plan, we went in daylight, and killed the yumens of Kelme Deva with arrows and hunting-lances, and burned their city and their engines. We left nothing. But that one had gone away. He came back alone. I sang over him, and let him go."

Selver fell silent.

"Then," Coro Mena whispered.

"Then a flying ship came from Sornol, and hunted us in the forest, but found nobody. So they set fire to the forest; but it rained, and they did little harm. Most of the people freed from the pens and the others have gone farther north and east, towards the Holle Hills, for we were afraid many yumens might come hunting us. I went alone. The yumens know me, you see, they know my face; and this frightens me, and those I stay with."

"What is your wound?" Torber asked.

"That one, he shot me with their kind of weapon; but I sang him down and let him go."

"Alone you downed a giant?" said Torber with a fierce grin, wishing to believe.

"Not alone. With three hunters, and with his weapon in my hand—this."

Torber drew back from the thing.

None of them spoke for a while. At last Coro Mena said, "What you tell us is very black, and the road goes down. Are you a Dreamer of your Lodge?"

"I was. There's no Lodge of Eshreth any more."

"That's all one; we speak the Old Tongue together. Among the willows of Asta you first spoke to me calling me Lord Dreamer. So I am. Do you dream, Selver?"

"Seldom now," Selver answered, obedient to the catechism, his scarred, feverish face bowed.

"Awake?"

"Awake."

"Do you dream well, Selver?"

"Not well."

"Do you hold the dream in your hands?"

"Yes."

"Do you weave and shape, direct and follow, start and cease at will?"

"Sometimes, not always."

"Can you walk the road your dream goes?"

"Sometimes. Sometimes I am afraid to."

"Who is not? It is not altogether bad with you, Selver."

"No, it is altogether bad," Selver said, "there's nothing good left," and he began to shake.

Torber gave him the willow-draught to drink and made him lie down. Coro Mena still had the headwoman's questions to ask; reluctantly he did so, kneeling by the sick man. "Will the giants, the yumens you call them, will they follow your trail, Selver?"

"I left no trail. No one has seen me between Kelme Deva and this place, six days. That's not the danger." He struggled to sit up again. "Listen, listen. You don't see the danger. How can you see it? You haven't done what I did, you have never dreamed of it, making two hundred people die. They will not follow me, but they may follow us all. Hunt us, as hunters drive coneys. That is the danger. They may try to kill us. To kill us all, all men."

"Lie down—"

"No, I'm not raving, this is true fact and dream. There were two hundred yumens at Kelme Deva and they are dead. We killed them. We killed them as if they were not men. So will they not turn and do the same? They have killed us by ones, now they will kill us as they kill the trees, by hundreds, and hundreds, and hundreds."

"Be still," Torber said. "Such things happen in the fever-dream, Selver. They do not happen in the world."

"The world is always new," said Coro Mena, "however old its roots. Selver, how is it with these creatures, then? They look like men and talk like men, are they not men?"

"I don't know. Do men kill men, except in madness? Does

any beast kill its own kind? Only the insects. These yumens kill us as lightly as we kill snakes. The one who taught me said that they kill one another, in quarrels, and also in groups, like ants fighting. I haven't seen that. But I know they don't spare one who asks life. They will strike a bowed neck, I have seen it! There is a wish to kill in them, and therefore I saw fit to put them to death."

"And all men's dreams," said Coro Mena, cross-legged in shadow, "will be changed. They will never be the same again. I shall never walk again that path I came with you yesterday, the way up from the willow grove that I've walked on all my life. It is changed. You have walked on it and it is utterly changed. Before this day the thing we had to do was the right thing to do; the way we had to go was the right way and led us home. Where is our home now? For you've done what you had to do, and it was not right. You have killed men. I saw them, five years ago, in the Lemgan Valley, where they came in a flying ship; I hid and watched the giants, six of them, and saw them speak, and look at rocks and plants, and cook food. They are men. But you have lived among them, tell me, Selver: do they dream?"

"As children do, in sleep."

"They have no training?"

"No. Sometimes they talk of their dreams, the healers try to use them in healing, but none of them are trained, or have any skill in dreaming. Lyubov, who taught me, understood me when I showed him how to dream, and yet even so he called the world-time 'real' and the dream-time 'unreal', as if that were the difference between them."

"You have done what you had to do," Coro Mena repeated after a silence. His eyes met Selver's, across shadows. The desperate tension lessened in Selver's face; his scarred mouth relaxed, and he lay back without saying more. In a little while he was asleep.

"He's a god," Coro Mena said.

Torber nodded, accepting the old man's judgment almost with relief.

"But not like the others. Not like the Pursuer, nor the Friend who has no face, nor the Aspen-leaf Woman who walks in the forest of dreams. He is not the Gatekeeper, nor the Snake. Nor the Lyre-player nor the Carver nor the Hunter, though he comes in the world-time like them. We may have dreamed of Selver these last few years, but we shall no longer; he has left the dream time. In the forest, through the forest he comes, where leaves fall, where trees fall, a god that knows death, a god that kills and is not himself reborn."

The headwoman listened to Coro Mena's reports and prophecies, and acted. She put the town of Cadast on alert, making sure that each family was ready to move out, with some food packed, and litters ready for the old and ill. She sent young women scouting south and east for news of the yumens. She kept one armed hunting-group always around town, though the others went out as usual every night. And when Selver grew stronger she insisted that he come out of the Lodge and tell his story: how the yumens killed an enslaved people in Sornol, and cut down the forests; how the people of Kelme Deva had killed the yumens. She forced women and undreaming men who did not understand these things to listen again, until they understood, and were frightened. For Ebor Dendep was a practical woman. When a Great Dreamer, her brother, told her that Selver was a god, a changer, a bridge between realities, she believed and acted. It was the Dreamer's responsibility to be careful, to be certain that his judgment was true. Her responsibility was then to take that judgment and act upon it. He saw what must be done; she saw that it was done.

"All the cities of the forest must hear," Coro Mena said. So the headwoman sent out her young runners, and headwomen in other towns listened, and sent out their runners. The killing at Kelme Deva and the name of Selver went over North Island and oversea to the other lands, from voice to voice, or in writing; not very fast, for the Forest People had no quicker messengers than footrunners; yet fast enough.

They were not all one people on the Forty Lands of the world. There were more languages than lands, and each with a different dialect for every town that spoke it; there were infinite ramifications of manners, morals, customs, crafts; physical types differed on each of the five Great Lands. The people of Sornol were tall, and pale, and great traders; the people of Rieshwel were short, and many had black fur, and they ate monkeys; and so on and on. But the climate varied little, and the forest little, and the sea not at all. Curiosity, regular trade-routes, and the necessity of finding a husband or wife of the proper Tree, kept up an easy movement of people among the towns and between the lands, and so there were certain likenesses among all but the remotest extremes, the half-rumoured barbarian isles of the Far East and South. In all the Forty Lands, women ran the cities and towns, and almost every town had a Men's Lodge. Within the Lodges the Dreamers spoke an old tongue, and this varied little from land to land. It was rarely learned by women or by men who remained hunters, fishers, weavers, builders, those who dreamed only small dreams outside the Lodge. As most writing was in this Lodge-tongue, when headwomen sent fleet girls carrying messages, the letters went from Lodge to Lodge, and so were interpreted by the Dreamers to the Old Women, as were other documents, rumours, problems, myths, and dreams. But it was always the Old Women's choice whether to believe or not.

Selver was in a small room at Eshsen. The door was not locked, but he knew if he opened it something bad would come in. So long as he kept it shut everything would be all right. The trouble was that there were young trees, a sapling orchard, planted out in front of the house; not fruit or nut trees but some other kind, he could not remember what kind. He went out to see what kind of trees they were. They all lay broken and uprooted. He picked up the silvery branch of one and a little blood ran out of the broken end. No, not

here, not again, Thele, he said: O Thele, come to me before
your death! But she did not come. Only her death was there,
the broken birchtree, the opened door. Selver turned and went
quickly back into the house, discovering that it was all built
above ground like a yumen house, very tall and full of
light. Outside the other door, across the tall room, was the
long street of the yumen city Central. Selver had the gun in
his belt. If Davidson came, he could shoot him. He waited,
just inside the open door, looking out into the sunlight.
Davidson came, huge, running so fast that Selver could
not keep him in the sights of the gun as he doubled crazily
back and forth across the wide street, very fast, always closer.
The gun was heavy. Selver fired it but no fire came out of it,
and in rage and terror he threw the gun and the dream away.

Disgusted and depressed, he spat, and sighed.

"A bad dream?" Ebor Dendep inquired.

"They're all bad, and all the same," he said, but the deep
unease and misery lessened a little as he answered. Cool
morning sunlight fell flecked and shafted through the fine
leaves and branches of the birch grove of Cadast. There
the headwoman sat weaving a basket of blackstem fern, for
she liked to keep her fingers busy, while Selver lay beside her
in half-dream and dream. He had been fifteen days at Cadast,
and his wound was healing well. He still slept much, but for
the first time in many months he had begun to dream waking
again, regularly, not once or twice in a day and night but
in the true pulse and rhythm of dreaming which should
rise and fall ten to fourteen times in the diurnal cycle. Bad
as his dreams were, all terror and shame, yet he welcomed
them. He had feared that he was cut off from his roots, that
he had gone too far into the dead land of action ever to
find his way back to the springs of reality. Now, though the
water was very bitter, he drank again.

Briefly he had Davidson down again among the ashes of
the burned camp, and instead of singing over him this time
he hit him in the mouth with a rock. Davidson's teeth broke,
and blood ran between the white splinters.

The dream was useful, a straight wish-fulfilment, but he stopped it there, having dreamed it many times, before he met Davidson in the ashes of Kelme Deva, and since. There was nothing to that dream but relief. A sip of bland water. It was the bitter he needed. He must go clear back, not to Kelme Deva but to the long dreadful street in the alien city called Central, where he had attacked Death, and had been defeated.

Ebor Dendep hummed as she worked. Her thin hands, their silky green down silvered with age, worked black fern-stems in and out, fast and neat. She sang a song about gathering ferns, a girl's song: I'm picking ferns, I wonder if he'll come back.... Her faint old voice trilled like a cricket's. Sun trembled in birch leaves. Selver put his head down on his arms.

The birch grove was more or less in the centre of the town of Cadast. Eight paths led away from it, winding narrowly off among trees. There was a whiff of woodsmoke in the air; where the branches were thin at the south edge of the grove you could see smoke rise from a house-chimney, like a bit of blue yarn unravelling among the leaves. If you looked closely among the live-oaks and other trees you would find houseroofs sticking up a couple of feet above ground, between a hundred and two hundred of them, it was very hard to count. The timber houses were three-quarters sunk, fitted in among tree-roots like badgers' setts. The beam roofs were mounded over with a thatch of small branches, pinestraw, reeds, earthmould. They were insulating, waterproof, almost invisible. The forest and the community of eight hundred people went about their business all around the birch grove where Ebor Dendep sat making a basket of fern. A bird among the branches over her head said, "Te-whet," sweetly. There was more people-noise than usual, for fifty or sixty strangers, young men and women mostly, had come drifting in these last few days, drawn by Selver's presence. Some were from other cities of the North, some were those who had done the killing at Kelme Deva with him; they had followed rumour here to follow him. Yet the voices calling here and there and the babble of women bathing or children playing down by the stream, were not so loud as the morning bird-song and insect-drone and under-noise of the living forest of which the town was one element.

A girl came quickly, a young huntress the colour of pale birch leaves. "Word of mouth from the southern coast, mother," she said. "The runner's at the Women's Lodge."

"Send her here when she's eaten," the headwoman said softly. "Sh, Tolbar, can't you see he's asleep?"

The girl stooped to pick a large leaf of wild tobacco, and laid it lightly over Selver's eyes, on which a shaft of the steepening, bright sunlight had fallen. He lay with his hands half open and his scarred, damaged face turned upward, vulnerable and foolish, a Great Dreamer gone to sleep like a child. But it was the girl's face that Ebor Dendep watched. It shone, in that uneasy shade, with pity and terror, with adoration.

Tolbar darted away. Presently two of the Old Women came with the messenger, moving silent in single file along the sun-flecked path. Ebor Dendep raised her hand, enjoining silence. The messenger promptly lay down flat, and rested; her brown-dappled green fur was dusty and sweaty, she had run far and fast. The Old Women sat down in patches of sun, and became still. Like two old grey-green stones they sat there, with bright living eyes.

Selver, struggling with a sleep-dream beyond his control, cried out as if in great fear, and woke.

He went to drink from the stream; when he came back he was followed by six or seven of those who always followed him. The headwoman put down her half-finished work and said, "Now be welcome, runner, and speak."

The runner stood up, bowed her head to Ebor Dendep, and spoke her message: "I come from Trethat. My words come from Sorbron Deva, before that from sailors of the Strait, before that from Broter in Sornol. They are for the hearing of all Cadast but they are to be spoken to the man called

Selver who was born of the Ash in Eshreth. Here are the words: There are new giants in the great city of the giants in Sornol, and many of these new ones are females. The yellow ship of fire goes up and down at the place that was called Peha. It is known in Sornol that Selver of Eshreth burned the city of the giants at Kelme Deva. The Great Dreamers of the Exiles in Broter have dreamed giants more numerous than the trees of the Forty Lands. These are all the words of the message I bear."

After the singsong recitation they were all silent. The bird, a little farther off, said, "Whet-whet?" experimentally.

"This is a very bad world-time," said one of the Old Women, rubbing a rheumatic knee.

A grey bird flew from a huge oak that marked the north edge of town, and went up in circles, riding the morning up-draught on lazy wings. There was always a roosting-tree of these grey kites near a town; they were the garbage service.

A small, fat boy ran through the birch grove, pursued by a slightly larger sister, both shrieking in tiny voices like bats. The boy fell down and cried, the girl stood him up and scrubbed his tears off with a large leaf. They scuttled off into the forest hand in hand.

"There was one called Lyubov," Selver said to the head-woman. "I have spoken of him to Coro Mena, but not to you. When that one was killing me, it was Lyubov who saved me. It was Lyubov who healed me, and set me free. He wanted to know about us; so I would tell him what he asked, and he too would tell me what I asked. Once I asked how his race could survive, having so few women. He said that in the place where they come from, half the race is women; but the men would not bring women to the Forty Lands until they had made a place ready for them."

"Until the men made a fit place for the women? Well! they may have quite a wait," said Ebor Dendep. "They're like the people in the Elm Dream who come at you rump-first, with their heads put on front to back. They make the forest into a dry beach"—her language had no word for "desert"—"and call that making things ready for the women? They should have sent the women first. Maybe with them the women do the Great Dreaming, who knows? They are backwards, Selver. They are insane."

"A people can't be insane."

"But they only dream in sleep, you said; if they want to dream waking they take poisons so that the dreams go out of control, you said! How can people be any madder? They don't know the dream-time from the world-time, any more than a baby does. Maybe when they kill a tree they think it will come alive again!"

Selver shook his head. He still spoke to the headwoman as if he and she were alone in the birch grove, in a quiet hesitant voice, almost drowsily. "No, they understand death very well.... Certainly they don't see as we do, but they know more and understand more about certain things than we do. Lyubov mostly understood what I told him. Much of what he told me, I couldn't understand. It wasn't the language that kept me from understanding; I know his tongue, and he learned ours; we made a writing of the two languages together. Yet there were things he said I could never understand. He said the yumens are from outside the forest. That's quite clear. He said they want the forest: the trees for wood, the land to plant grass on." Selver's voice, though still soft, had taken on resonance; the people among the silver trees listened. "That too is clear, to those of us who've seen them cutting down the world. He said the yumens are men like us, that we're indeed related, as close kin maybe as the Red Deer to the Greybuck. He said that they come from another place which is not the forest; the trees there are all cut down; it has a sun, not our sun, which is a star. All this, as you see, wasn't clear to me. I say his words but don't know what they mean. It does not matter much. It is clear that they want our forest for themselves. They are twice our stature, they have weapons that outshoot ours by far, and fire-throwers, and flying-ships. Now they have brought more women, and will have children. There are maybe two thousand, maybe three thousand of them here now, mostly in Sornol. But if we wait a lifetime or two they will breed; their numbers will double and redouble. They kill men and women; they do not spare those who ask life. They cannot sing in contest. They have left their roots behind them, perhaps, in this other forest from which they came, this forest with no trees. So they take poison to let loose the dreams in them, but it only makes them drunk or sick. No one can say certainly whether they're men or not men, whether they're sane or insane, but that does not matter. They must be made to leave the forest, because they are dangerous. If they will not go they must be burned out of the Lands, as nests of stinging-ants must be burned out of the groves of cities. If we wait, it is we that will be smoked out and burned. They can step on us as we step on stinging-ants. Once I saw a woman, it was when they burned my city Eshreth, she lay down in the path before a yumen to ask him for life, and he stepped on her back and broke the spine, and then kicked her aside as if she was a dead snake. I saw that. If the yumens are men they are men unfit or untaught to dream and to act as men. Therefore they go about in torment killing and destroying, driven by the gods within, whom they will not set free but try to uproot and deny. If they are men they are evil men, having denied their own gods, afraid to see their own faces in the dark. Headwoman of Cadast, hear me." Selver stood up, tall and abrupt among the seated women. "It's time, I think, that I go back to my own land, to Sornol, to those that are in exile and those that are enslaved. Tell any people who dream of a city burning to come after me to Broter." He bowed to Ebor Dendep and left the birch grove, still walking lame, his arm bandaged; yet there was a quickness to his walk, a poise to his head, that made him seem more whole than other men. The young people followed quietly after him.

"Who is he?" asked the runner from Trethat, her eyes following him.

"The man to whom your message came, Selver of Eshreth,

a god among us. Have you ever seen a god before, daughter?"

"When I was ten the Lyre-Player came to our town."

"Old Ertel, yes. He was of my Tree, and from the North Vales like me. Well, now you've seen a second god, and a greater. Tell your people in Trethat of him."

"Which god is he, mother?"

"A new one," Ebor Dendep said in her dry old voice. "The son of forest-fire, the brother of the murdered. He is the one who is not reborn. Now go on, all of you, go on to the Lodge. See who'll be going with Selver, see about food for them to carry. Let me be a while. I'm as full of forebodings as a stupid old man, I must dream. . . ."

Coro Mena went with Selver that night as far as the place where they first met, under the copper willows by the stream. Many people were following Selver south, some sixty in all, as great a troop as most people had ever seen on the move at once. They would cause great stir and thus gather many more to them, on their way to the sea-crossing to Sornol. Selver had claimed his Dreamer's privilege of solitude for this one night. He was setting off alone. His followers would catch him up in the morning; and thenceforth, implicated in crowd and act, he would have little time for the slow and deep running of great dreams.

"Here we met," the old man said, stopping among the bowing branches, the veils of dropping leaves, "and here part. This will be called Selver's Grove, no doubt, by the people who walk our paths hereafter."

Selver said nothing for a while, standing still as a tree, the restless leaves about him darkening from silver as clouds thickened over the stars. "You are surer of me than I am," he said at last, a voice in darkness.

"Yes, I'm sure, Selver. . . . I was well taught in dreaming, and then I'm old. I dream very little for myself any more. Why should I? Little is new to me. And what I wanted from my life, I have had, and more. I have had my whole life. Days like the leaves of the forest. I'm an old hollow tree, only the roots live. And so I dream only what all men dream. I have no visions and no wishes. I see what is. I see the fruit ripening on the branch. Four years it has been ripening, that fruit of the deep-planted tree. We have all been afraid for four years, even we who live far from the yumens' cities, and have only glimpsed them from hiding, or seen their ships fly over, or looked at the dead places where they cut down the world, or heard mere tales of these things. We are all afraid. Children wake from sleep crying of giants; women will not go far from their trading-journeys; men in the Lodges cannot sing. The fruit of fear is ripening. And I see you gather it. You are the harvester. All that we fear to know, you have seen, you have known: exile, shame, pain, the roof and walls of the world fallen, the mother dead in misery, the children untaught, uncherished.... This is a new time for the world: a bad time. And you have suffered it all. You have gone farthest. And at the farthest, at the end of the black path, there grows the Tree; there the fruit ripens; now you reach up, Selver, now you gather it. And the world changes wholly, when a man holds in his hand the fruit of that tree, whose roots are deeper than the forest. Men will know it. They will know you, as we did. It doesn't take an old man or a Great Dreamer to recognise a god! Where you go, fire burns; only the blind cannot see it. But listen, Selver, this is what I see that perhaps others do not, this is why I have loved you: I dreamed of you before we met here. You were walking on a path, and behind you the young trees grew up, oak and birch, willow and holly, fir and pine, alder, elm, white-flowering ash, all the roof and walls of the world, forever renewed. Now farewell, dear god and son, go safely."

The night darkened as Selver went, until even his night-seeing eyes saw nothing but masses and planes of black. It began to rain. He had gone only a few miles from Cadast when he must either light a torch, or halt. He chose to halt, and groping found a place among the roots of a great chestnut tree. There he sat, his back against the broad, twisting bole that seemed to hold a little sun-warmth in it still. The fine rain, falling unseen in darkness, pattered on the leaves overhead, on his arms and neck and head protected by their silk-fine hair, on the earth and ferns and undergrowth nearby, on all the leaves of the forest, near and far. Selver sat as quiet as the grey owl on a branch above him, unsleeping, his eyes wide open in the rainy dark.

CHAPTER THREE

Captain Raj Lyubov had a headache. It began softly in the muscles of his right shoulder, and mounted crescendo to a smashing drumbeat over his right ear. The speech centres are in the left cerebral cortex, he thought, but he couldn't have said it; couldn't speak, or read, or sleep, or think. Cortex, vortex. Migraine headache, margarine breadache, ow, ow, ow. Of course he had been cured of migraine once at college and again during his obligatory Army Prophylactic Psychotherapy Sessions, but he had brought along some ergotamine pills when he left Earth, just in case. He had taken two, and a superhyperduper-analgesic, and a tranquilliser, and a digestive pill to counteract the caffeine which counteracted the ergotamine, but the awl still bored out from within, just over his right ear, to the beat of the big bass drum. Awl, drill, ill, pill, oh God. Lord deliver us. Liver sausage. What would the Athsheans do for a migraine? They wouldn't have one, they would have daydreamed the tensions away a week before they got them. Try it, try daydreaming. Begin as Selver taught you. Although knowing nothing of electricity he could not really grasp the principle of the EEG, as soon as he heard about alpha waves and when they appear he had said, "Oh yes, you mean this," and there appeared the unmistakable alpha-squiggles on the graph recording what went on inside his small green head; and he had taught Lyubov how to turn on and off the alpha-rhythms in one half-hour lesson. There really was nothing to it. But not now, the world is too much with us, ow, ow, ow above the right ear I always hear Time's winged chariot hurrying near, for the Athsheans had burned Smith Camp day before yesterday and killed two hundred men. Two hundred and seven to be precise. Every man alive except the Captain. No wonder pills couldn't get at the centre of his migraine, for it was on an island two hundred miles away two days ago. Over the hills and far away. Ashes, ashes, all fall down. And amongst the ashes, all his knowledge of the High Intelligence Life Forms of World 41. Dust, rubbish, a mess of false data and fake hypotheses. Nearly five E-years here, and he had believed the Athsheans to be incapable of killing men, his kind or their kind. He had written long papers to explain how and why they couldn't kill men. All wrong. Dead wrong.

What had he failed to see?

It was nearly time to be going over to the meeting at HQ. Cautiously Lyubov stood up, moving all in one piece so that the right side of his head would not fall off; he approached his desk with the gait of a man underwater, poured out a shot of General Issue vodka, and drank it. It turned him inside out: it extraverted him: it normalised him. He felt better. He went out, and unable to stand the jouncing of his motorbike, started to walk down the long dusty main street of Centralville to HQ. Passing the Luau he thought with greed of another vodka; but Captain Davidson was just going in the door, and Lyubov went on.

The people from the *Shackleton* were already in the conference room. Commander Yung, whom he had met before, had brought some new faces down from orbit this time. They were not in Navy uniform; after a moment Lyubov recognised them, with a slight shock, as non-Terran humans. He sought an introduction at once. One, Mr Or, was a Hairy Cetian, dark grey, stocky, and dour; the other, Mr Lepennon, was tall, white, and comely: a Hainishman. They greeted Lyubov with interest, and Lepennon said, "I've just been reading your report on the conscious control of paradoxical sleep among the Athsheans, Dr Lyubov," which was pleasant, and it was pleasant also to be called by his own, earned title of doctor. Their conversation indicated that they had spent some years on Earth, and that they might be hilfers, or something like it; but the Commander, introducing them, had not mentioned their status or position.

The room was filling up. Gosse, the colony ecologist, came in; so did all the high brass; so did Captain Susun, head of Planet Development—logging operations—whose captaincy like Lyubov's was an invention necessary to the peace of the military mind. Captain Davidson came in alone, straight-backed and handsome, his lean, rugged face calm and rather stern. Guards stood at all the doors. The Army necks were all stiff as crowbars. The conference was plainly an Investigation. *Whose fault?* My fault, Lyubov thought despairingly; but out of his despair he looked across the table at Captain Don Davidson with detestation and contempt.

Commander Yung had a very quiet voice. "As you know, gentlemen, my ship stopped here at World 41 to drop you off a new load of colonists, and nothing more; *Shackleton*'s mission is to World 88, Prestno, one of the Hainish Group. How-ever, this attack on your outpost camp, since it chanced to occur during our week here, can't be simply ignored; par-ticularly in the light of certain developments which you would have been informed of a little later, in the normal course of events. The fact is that the status of World 41 as an Earth Colony is now subject to revision, and the massacre at your camp may precipitate the Administration's decisions on it. Certainly the decisions *we* can make must be made quickly, for I can't keep my ship here long. Now first, we wish to make sure that the relevant facts are all in the possession of those present. Captain Davidson's report on the events at Smith Camp was taped and heard by all of us on ship; by all of you here also? Good. Now if there are questions any of you wish to ask Captain Davidson, go ahead. I have one myself. You returned to the site of the camp the following day, Captain Davidson, in a large hopper with eight soldiers; had you the permission of a senior officer here at Central for that flight?"

Davidson stood up. "I did, sir."

"Were you authorised to land and to set fires in the forest near the campsite?"

"No, sir."

"You did, however, set fires?"

"I did, sir. I was trying to smoke out the creechies that killed my men."

"Very well. Mr Lepennon?"

The tall Hainishman cleared his throat. "Captain Davidson," he said, "do you think that the people under your command at Smith Camp were mostly content?"

"Yes, I do."

Davidson's manner was firm and forthright; he seemed indifferent to the fact that he was in trouble. Of course these Navy officers and foreigners had no authority over him; it was to his own Colonel that he must answer for losing two hundred men and making unauthorised reprisals. But his Colonel was right there, listening.

"They were well fed, well housed, not overworked, then, as well as can be managed in a frontier camp?"

"Yes."

"Was the discipline maintained very harsh?"

"No, it was not."

"What, then, do you think motivated the revolt?"

"I don't understand."

"If none of them were discontented, why did some of them massacre the rest and destroy the camp?"

There was a worried silence.

"May I put in a word," Lyubov said. "It was the native hilfs, the Athsheans employed in the camp, who joined with an attack by the forest people against the Terran humans. In his report Captain Davidson referred to the Athsheans as 'creechies'."

Lepennon looked embarrassed and anxious. "Thank you, Dr Lyubov. I misunderstood entirely. Actually I took the word 'creechie' to stand for a Terran caste that did rather menial work in the logging camps. Believing, as we all did, that the Athsheans were intraspecies non-aggressive, I never thought they might be the group meant. In fact I didn't realise that they cooperated with you in your camps— However, I am more at a loss than ever to understand what provoked the attack and mutiny."

"I don't know, sir."

"When he said the people under his command were content, did the Captain include native people?" said the Cetian, Or, in a dry mumble. The Hainishman picked it up at once, and asked Davidson, in his concerned, courteous voice, "Were the Athsheans living at the camp content, do you think?"

"So far as I know."

"There was nothing unusual in their position there, or the work they had to do?"

Lyubov felt the heightening of tension, one turn of the screw, in Colonel Dongh and his staff, and also in the starship commander. Davidson remained calm and easy. "Nothing unusual."

Lyubov knew now that only his scientific studies had been sent up to the *Shackleton*; his protests, even his annual assessments of "Native Adjustment to Colonial Presence" required by the Administration, had been kept in some desk drawer deep in HQ. These two N.-T.H.'s knew nothing about the exploitation of the Athsheans. Commander Yung did, of course; he had been down before today and had probably seen the creechie-pens. In any case a Navy commander on Colony runs wouldn't have much to learn about Terran-hilf relations. Whether or not he approved of how the Colonial Administration ran its business, not much would come as a shock to him. But a Cetian and a Hainishman, how much would they know about Terran colonies, unless chance brought them to one on the way to somewhere else? Lepennon and Or had not intended to come on-planet here at all. Or possibly they had not been intended to come on-planet, but, hearing of trouble, had insisted. Why had the commander brought them down: his will, or theirs? Whoever they were they had about them a hint of authority, a whiff of the dry, intoxicating odour of power. Lyubov's headache had gone, he felt alert and excited, his face was rather hot. "Captain Davidson," he said, "I have a couple of questions, concerning your confrontation with the four natives, day before yesterday. You're certain that one of them was Sam, or Selver Thele?"

"I believe so."

"You're aware that he has a personal grudge against you."

"I don't know."

"You don't? Since his wife died in your quarters immediately subsequent to sexual intercourse with you, he holds you responsible for her death; you didn't know that? He attacked you once before, here in Centralville; you had forgotten that? Well, the point is, that Selver's personal hatred for Captain Davidson may serve as a partial explanation or motivation for this unprecedented assault. The Athsheans aren't incapable of personal violence, that's never been asserted in any of my studies of them. Adolescents who haven't mastered controlled dreaming or competitive singing do a lot of wrestling and fist-fighting, not all of it good-tempered. But Selver is an adult and an adept; and his first, personal attack on Captain Davidson, which I happened to witness part of, was pretty certainly an attempt to kill. As was the Captain's retaliation, incidentally. At the time, I thought that atttack an isolated psychotic incident, resulting from grief and stress, not likely to be repeated. I was wrong— Captain, when the four Athsheans jumped you from ambush, as you describe in your report, did you end up prone on the ground?"

"Yes."

"In what position?"

Davidson's calm face tensed and stiffened, and Lyubov felt a pang of compunction. He wanted to corner Davidson in his lies, to force him into speaking truth once, but not to humiliate him before others. Accusations of rape and murder supported Davidson's image of himself as the totally virile man, but now that image was endangered: Lyubov had called up a picture of him, the soldier, the fighter, the cool tough man, being knocked down by enemies the size of six-year-olds.... What did it cost Davidson, then, to recall that moment when he had lain looking up at the little green men, for once, not down at them?

"I was on my back."

"Was your head thrown back, or turned aside?"

"I don't know."

"I'm trying to establish a fact here, Captain, one that might help explain why Selver didn't kill you, although he had a grudge against you and had helped kill two hundred men a few hours earlier. I wondered if you might by chance have been in one of the positions which, when assumed by an Athshean, prevent his opponent from further physical aggression."

"I don't know."

Lyubov glanced round the conference table; all the faces showed curiosity and some tension. "These aggression-halting gestures and positions may have some innate basis, may rise from a surviving trigger-response, but they are socially developed and expanded, and of course learned. The strongest and completest of them is a prone position, on the back, eyes shut, head turned so the throat is fully exposed. I think an Athshean of the local cultures might find it impossible to hurt an enemy who took that position. He would have to do something else to release his anger or aggressive drive— When they had all got you down, Captain, did Selver by any chance sing?"

"Did he what?"

"Sing."

"I don't know."

Block. No go. Lyubov was about to shrug and give it up when the Cetian said. "Why, Mr Lyubov?" The most winning characteristic of the rather harsh Cetian temperament was curiosity, inopportune and inexhaustible curiosity; Cetians died eagerly, curious as to what came next.

"You see," Lyubov said, "the Athsheans use a kind of ritualised singing to replace physical combat. Again it's a universal social phenomenon that might have a physiological foundation, though it's very hard to establish anything as 'innate' in human beings. However the higher primates here all go in for vocal competing between two males, a lot of howling and whistling; the dominant male may finally give the other a cuff, but usually they just spend an hour or so trying to outbellow each other. The Athsheans themselves see the similarity to their singing-matches, which are also only between males; but as they observe, theirs are not only aggression-releases, but an art-form. The better artist wins. I wondered if Selver sang over Captain Davidson, and if so, whether he did because he could not kill, or because he preferred the bloodless victory. These questions have suddenly become rather urgent."

"Dr Lyubov," said Lepennon, "how effective are these aggression-channelling devices? Are they universal?"

"Among adults, yes. So my informants state, and all my observation supported them, until day before yesterday. Rape, violent assault, and murder virtually don't exist among them. There are accidents, of course. And there are psychotics. Not many of the latter."

"What do they do with dangerous psychotics?"

"Isolate them. Literally. On small islands."

"The Athsheans are carnivorous, they hunt animals?"

"Yes, meat is a staple."

"Wonderful," Lepennon said, and his white skin paled further with pure excitement, "A human society with an effective war-barrier! What's the cost, Dr Lyubov?"

"I'm not sure, Mr Lepennon. Perhaps change. They're a static, stable, uniform society. They have no history. Perfectly integrated, and wholly unprogressive. You might say that like the forest they live in, they've attained a climax state. But I don't mean to imply that they're incapable of adaptation."

"Gentlemen, this is very interesting but in a somewhat specialist frame of reference, and it may be somewhat out of the context which we're attempting to clarify here—"

"No, excuse me, Colonel Dongh, this may be the point. Yes, Dr Lyubov?"

"Well, I wonder if they're not proving their adaptability, now. By adapting their behaviour to us. To the Earth Colony. For four years they've behaved to us as they do to one another. Despite the physical differences, they recognised us as members of their species, as men. However, we have not responded as members of their species should respond. We have ignored the responses, the rights and obligations of non-violence. We have killed, raped, dispersed, and enslaved the native humans, destroyed their communities, and cut down their forests. It wouldn't be surprising if they'd decided that we are not human."

"And therefore can be killed, like animals, yes yes," said the Cetian, enjoying logic; but Lepennon's face now was stiff as white stone. "Enslaved?" he said.

"Captain Lyubov is expressing his personal opinions and theories," said Colonel Dongh, "which I should state I consider possibly to be erroneous, and he and I have discussed this type of thing previously, although the present context is unsuitable. We do not employ slaves, sir. Some of the natives serve a useful role in our community. The Voluntary Autochthonous Labour Corps is a part of all but the temporary camps here. We have very limited personnel to accomplish our tasks here and we need workers and use all we can get, but on any kind of basis that could be called a slavery basis, certainly not."

Lepennon was about to speak, but deferred to the Cetian, who said only, "How many of each race?"

Gosse replied: "2641 Terrans, now. Lyubov and I estimate the native hilf population very roughly at 3 million."

"You should have considered these statistics, gentlemen, before you altered the native traditions!" said Or, with a disagreeable but perfectly genuine laugh.

"We are adequately armed and equipped to resist any type of aggression these natives could offer," said the Colonel. "However there was a general consensus by both the first

Exploratory Missions and our own research staff of specialists here headed by Captain Lyubov, giving us to understand that the New Tahitians are a primitive, harmless,
peace-loving species. Now this information, was obviously
erroneous—"

Or interrupted the Colonel. "Obviously! You consider
the human species to be primitive, harmless, and peace-
loving, Colonel? No. But you knew that the hilfs of this
planet are human? As human as you or I or Lepennon—
since we all came from the same, original, Hainish stock?"

"That is the scientific theory, I am aware—"

"Colonel, it is the historic fact."

"I am not forced to accept it as a fact," the old Colonel
said, getting hot, "and I don't like opinions stuffed into my
own mouth. The fact is that these creechies are a metre tall,
they're covered with green fur, they don't sleep, and they're
not human beings in my frame of reference!"

"Captain Davidson," said the Cetian, "do you consider the
native hilfs human, or not?"

"I don't know."

"But you had sexual intercourse with one—this Selver's
wife. Would you have sexual intercourse with a female
animal? What about the rest of you?" He looked about at the
purple colonel, the glowering majors, the livid captains, the
cringing specialists. Contempt came into his face. "You have
not thought things through," he said. By his standards it was
a brutal insult.

The Commander of the *Shackleton* at last salvaged words
from the gulf of embarrassed silence. "Well, gentlemen, the
tragedy at Smith Camp clearly is involved with the entire
colony-native relationship, and is not by any means an insig-
nificant or isolated episode. That's what we had to establish.
And this being the case, we can make a certain contribution
towards easing your problems here. The main purpose of our
journey was not to drop off a couple of hundred girls here,
though I know you've been waiting for 'em, but to get to
Prestno, which has been having some difficulties, and give the

government there an ansible. That is, an ICD transmitter."

"What?" said Sereng, an engineer. Stares became fixed, all round the table.

"The one we have aboard is an early model, and it cost a planetary annual revenue, roughly. That, of course, was 27 years ago planetary time, when we left Earth. Nowadays they're making them relatively cheaply; they're SI on Navy ships; and in the normal course of things a robo or manned ship would be coming out here to give your colony one. As a matter of fact it's a manned Administration ship, and is on the way, due here in 9.4 E-years if I recall the figure."

"How do you know that?" somebody said, setting it up for Commander Yung, who replied smiling, "By the ansible: the one we have aboard. Mr Or, your people invented the device, perhaps you'd explain it to those here who are unfamiliar with the terms?"

The Cetian did not unbend. "I shall not attempt to explain the principles of ansible operation to those present," he said. "Its effect can be stated simply: the instantaneous transmission of a message over any distance. One element must be on a large-mass body, the other can be anywhere in the cosmos. Since arrival in orbit the *Shackleton* has been in daily communication with Terra, now 27 lightyears distant. The message does not take 54 years for delivery and response, as it does on an electromagnetic device. It takes no time. There is no more time-gap between worlds."

"As soon as we came out of NAFAL time-dilatation into planetary space-time, here, we rang up home, as you might say," the soft-voiced Commander went on. "And were told what had happened during the 27 years we were travelling. The time-gap for bodies remains, but the information lag does not. As you can see, this is as important to us as an interstellar species, as speech itself was to us earlier in our evolution. It'll have the same effect: to make a society possible."

"Mr Or and I left Earth, 27 years ago, as Legates for our respective governments, Tau II and Hain," said Lepennon. His voice was still gentle and civil, but the warmth had gone out of it. "When we left, people were talking about the possibility of forming some kind of league among the civilised worlds, now that communication was possible. The League of Worlds now exists. It has existed for 18 years. Mr Or and I are now Emissaries of the Council of the League, and so have certain powers and responsibilities we did not have when we left Earth."

The three of them from the ship kept saying these things: an instantaneous communicator exists, an interstellar super-government exists.... Believe it or not. They were in league, and lying. This thought went through Lyubov's mind; he considered it, decided it was a reasonable but unwarranted suspicion, a defence-mechanism, and discarded it. Some of the military staff, however, trained to compartmentalise their thinking, specialists in self-defence, would accept it as un-hesitatingly as he discarded it. They must believe that any-one claiming a sudden new authority was a liar or conspirator. They were no more constrained than Lyubov, who had been trained to keep his mind open whether he wanted to or not.

"Are we to take all—all this simply on your word, sir?" said Colonel Dongh, with dignity and some pathos; for he, too muddleheaded to compartmentalise neatly, knew that he shouldn't believe Lepennon and Or and Yung, but did believe them, and was frightened.

"No," said the Cetian. "That's done with. A colony like this had to believe what passing ships and outdated radio-messages told them. Now you don't. You can verify. We are going to give you the ansible destined for Prestno. We have League authority to do so. Received, of course, by ansible. Your colony here is in a bad way. Worse than I thought from your reports. Your reports are very incomplete; censorship or stupidity have been at work. Now, however, you'll have the ansible, and can talk with your Terran Administration; you can ask for orders, so you'll know how to proceed. Given the profound changes that have been occurring in the organ-isation of the Terran Government since we left there, I should recommend that you do so at once. There is no longer any excuse for acting on outdated orders; for ignorance; for irresponsible autonomy."

Sour a Cetian and, like milk, he stayed sour. Mr Or was being overbearing, and Commander Yung should shut him up. But could he? How did an "Emissary of the Council of the League of Worlds" rank? Who's in charge here, thought Lyubov, and he too felt a qualm of fear. His headache had returned as a sense of constriction, a sort of tight headband over the temples.

He looked across the table at Lepennon's white, long-fingered hands, lying left over right, quiet, on the bare polished wood of the table. The white skin was a defect to Lyubov's Earth-formed aesthetic taste, but the serenity and strength of those hands pleased him very much. To the Hainish, he thought, civilisation came naturally. They had been at it so long. They lived the social-intellectual life with the grace of a cat hunting in a garden, the certainty of a swallow following summer over the sea. They were experts. They never had to pose, to fake. They were what they were. Nobody seemed to fit the human skin so well. Except, perhaps, the little green men? the deviant, dwarfed, over-adapted, stagnated creechies, who were as absolutely, as honestly, as serenely what they were....

An officer, Benton, was asking Lepennon if he and Or were on this planet as observers for the (he hesitated) League of Worlds, or if they claimed any authority to ... Lepennon took him up politely: "We are observers here, not empowered to command, only to report. You are still answerable only to your own government on Earth."

Colonel Dongh said with relief, "Then nothing has essentially changed—"

"You forget the ansible," Or interrupted. "I'll instruct you in its operation, Colonel, as soon as this discussion is over. You can then consult with your Colonial Administration."

"Since your problem here is rather urgent, and since Earth is now a League member and may have changed the Colonial Code somewhat during recent years, Mr Or's advice is both

proper and timely. We should be very grateful to Mr Or and
Mr Lepennon for their decision to give this Terran colony
the ansible destined for Prestno. It was their decision; I can
only applaud it. Now, one more decision remains to be made,
and this one I have to make, using your judgment as my
guide. If you feel the colony is in imminent peril of further
and more massive attacks from the natives, I can keep my
ship here for a week or two as a defence arsenal; I can also
evacuate the women. No children yet, right?"

"No, sir," said Gosse. "482 women, now."

"Well, I have space for 380 passengers; we might crowd a
hundred more in; the extra mass would add a year or so to
the trip home, but it could be done. Unfortunately that's all
I can do. We must proceed to Prestno; your nearest neigh-
bour, as you know, 1.8 lightyears distant. We'll stop here on
the way home to Terra, but that's going to be three and a
half more E-years at least. Can you stick it out?"

"Yes," said the Colonel, and others echoed him. "We've had
warning now and we won't be caught napping again."

"Equally," said the Cetian, "can the native inhabitants
stick it out for three and a half Earth-years more?"

"Yes," said the Colonel. "No," said Lyubov. He had been
watching Davidson's face, and a kind of panic had taken hold
of him.

"Colonel?" said Lepennon, politely.

"We've been here four years now and the natives are
flourishing. There's room enough and to spare for all of us,
as you can see the planet's heavily underpopulated and the
Administration wouldn't have cleared it for colonisation pur-
poses if that hadn't been as it is. As for if this entered anyone's
head, they won't catch us off guard again, we were erron-
eously briefed concerning the nature of these natives, but
we're fully armed and able to defend ourselves, but we aren't
planning any reprisals. That is expressly forbidden in the
Colonial Code, though I don't know what new rules this new
government may have added on, but we'll just stick to our
own as we have been doing and they definitely negative mass

reprisals or genocide. We won't be sending any messages for help out, after all a colony 27 lightyears from home has come out expecting to be on its own and to in fact be completely self-sufficient, and I don't see that the ICD really changes that, due to ship and men and material still have to travel at near lightspeed. We'll just keep on shipping the lumber home, and look out for ourselves. The women are in no danger."

"Mr Lyubov?" said Lepennon.

"We've been here four years. I don't know if the native human culture will survive four more. As for the total land ecology, I think Gosse will back me if I say that we've irrecoverably wrecked the native life-systems on one large island, have done great damage on this subcontinent Sornol, and if we go on logging at the present rate, may reduce the major habitable lands to desert within ten years. This isn't the fault of the colony's HQ or Forestry Bureau; they've simply been following a Development Plan drawn up on Earth without sufficient knowledge of the planet to be exploited, its life-systems, or its native human inhabitants."

"Mr Gosse?" said the polite voice.

"Well, Raj, you're stretching things a bit. There's no denying that Dump Island, which was overlogged in direct contravention to my recommendations, is a dead loss. If more than a certain percentage of the forest is cut over a certain area, then the fibreweed doesn't reseed, you see, gentlemen, and the fibreweed root-system is the main soil-binder on clear land; without it the soil goes dusty and drifts off very fast under wind-erosion and the heavy rainfall. But I can't agree that our basic directives are at fault, so long as they're scrupulously followed. They were based on careful study of the planet. We've succeeded, here on Central, by following the Plan: erosion is minimal, and the cleared soil is highly arable. To log off a forest doesn't, after all, mean to make a desert—except perhaps from the point of view of a squirrel. We can't forecast precisely how the native forest life-systems will adapt to the new woodland-prairie-ploughland ambiance foreseen in the Development Plan, but we know the chances are good for a large percentage of adaptation and survival."

"That's what the Bureau of Land Management said about Alaska during the First Famine," said Lyubov. His throat had tightened so that his voice came out high and husky. He had counted on Gosse for support. "How many Sitka spruce have you seen in your lifetime, Gosse? Or snowy owl? or wolf? or Eskimo? The survival percentage of native Alaskan species in habitat, after 15 years of the Development Programme, was .3%. It's now zero— A forest ecology is a delicate one. If the forest perishes, its fauna may go with it. The Athshean word for *world* is also the word for *forest*. I submit, Commander Yung, that though the colony may not be in imminent danger, the planet is—"

"Captain Lyubov," said the old Colonel, "such submissions are not properly submitted by staff specialist officers to officers of other branches of the service but should rest on the judgment of the senior officers of the Colony, and I cannot tolerate any further such attempts as this to give advice without previous clearance."

Caught off guard by his own outburst, Lyubov apologised and tried to look calm. If only he didn't lose his temper, if his voice didn't go weak and husky, if he had poise. . . .

The Colonel went on. "It appears to us that you made some serious erroneous judgments concerning the peacefulness and non-aggressiveness of the natives here, and because we counted on this specialist description of them as non-aggressive is why we left ourselves open to this terrible tragedy at Smith Camp, Captain Lyubov. So I think we have to wait until some other specialists in hilfs have had time to study them, because evidently your theories were basically erroneous to some extent."

Lyubov sat and took it. Let the men from the ship see them all passing the blame around like a hot brick : all the better. The more dissension they showed, the likelier were these Emissaries to have them checked and watched over. And he was to blame; he had been wrong. To hell with my self-respect so long as the forest people get a chance, Lyubov thought, and so strong a sense of his own humiliation and self-sacrifice came over him that tears rose to his eyes.

He was aware that Davidson was watching him.

He sat up stiff, the blood hot in his face, his temples drumming. He would not be sneered at by that bastard Davidson. Couldn't Or and Lepennon see what kind of man Davidson was, and how much power he had here, while Lyubov's powers, called "advisory", were simply derisory? If the colonists were left to go on with no check on them but a super-radio, the Smith Camp massacre would almost certainly become the excuse for systematic aggression against the natives. Bacteriological extermination, most likely. The *Shackleton* would come back in three and a half or four years to "New Tahiti", and find a thriving Terran colony, and no more Creechie Problem. None at all. Pity about the plague, we took all precautions required by the Code, but it must have been some kind of mutation, they had no natural resistance, but we did manage to save a group of them by transporting them to the New Falkland Isles in the southern hemisphere and they're doing fine there, all sixty-two of them. . . .

The conference did not last much longer. When it ended he stood up and leaned across the table to Lepennon. "You must tell the League to do something to save the forests, the forest people," he said almost inaudibly, his throat constricted, "you must, please, you must."

The Hainishman met his eyes; his gaze was reserved, kindly, and deep as a well. He said nothing.

CHAPTER FOUR

It was unbelievable. They'd all gone insane. This damned alien world had sent them all right round the bend, into byebye dreamland, along with the creechies. He still wouldn't believe what he'd seen at that "conference" and the briefing after it, if he saw it all over again on film. A Starfleet ship's commander bootlicking two humanoids. Engineers and techs cooing and ooing over a fancy radio presented to them by a Hairy Cetian with a lot of sneering and boasting, as if ICDs hadn't been predicted by Terran science years ago! The humanoids had stolen the idea, implemented it, and called it an "ansible" so nobody would realise it was just an ICD. But the worst part of it had been the conference, with that psycho Lyubov raving and crying, and Colonel Dongh letting him do it, letting him insult Davidson and HQ staff and the whole Colony; and all the time the two aliens sitting and grinning, the little grey ape and the big white fairy, sneering at humans.

It had been pretty bad. It hadn't got any better since the *Shackleton* left. He didn't mind being sent down to New Java Camp under Major Muhamed. The Colonel had to discipline him; old Ding Dong might actually be very happy about that fire-raid he'd pulled in reprisal on Smith Island, but the raid had been a breach of discipline and he had to reprimand Davidson. All right, rules of the game. But what wasn't in the rules was this stuff coming over that overgrown TV set they called the ansible—their new little tin god at HQ.

Orders from the Bureau of Colonial Administration in Karachi: *Restrict Terran-Athshean contact to occasions ar-*

ranged by Athsheans. In other words you couldn't go into a creechie warren and round up a work-force any more. *Employment of volunteer labour is not advised; employment of forced labour is forbidden.* More of same. How the hell were they supposed to get the work done? Did Earth want this wood or didn't it? They were still sending the robot cargo ships to New Tahiti, weren't they, four a year, each carrying about 30 million new-dollars' worth of prime lumber back to Mother Earth. Sure the Development people wanted those millions. They were businessmen. These messages weren't coming from them, any fool could see that.

The colonial status of World 41—why didn't they call it New Tahiti any more?—*is under consideration. Until decision is reached colonists should observe extreme caution in all dealings with native inhabitants. . . . The use of weapons of any kind except small side-arms carried in self-defence is absolutely forbidden*—just as on Earth, except that there a man couldn't even carry side-arms any more. But what the hell was the use coming 27 lightyears to a frontier world and then get told No guns, no firejelly, no bugbombs, no no, just sit like nice little boys and let the creechies come spit in your faces and sing songs at you and then stick a knife in your guts and burn down your camp, but don't you hurt the cute little green fellers, no sir!

A policy of avoidance is strongly advised; a policy of aggression or retaliation is strictly forbidden.

That was the gist of all the messages actually, and any fool could tell that that wasn't the Colonial Administration talking. They couldn't have changed that much in thirty years. They were practical, realistic men who knew what life was like on frontier planets. It was clear, to anybody who hadn't gone spla from geoshock, that the "ansible" messages were phoneys. They might be planted right in the machine, a whole set of answers to high-probability questions, computer run. The engineers said they could have spotted that; maybe so. In that case the thing did communicate instantaneously with another world. But that world wasn't Earth.

Not by a long long shot! There weren't any men typing the
answers onto the other end of that little trick: they were
aliens, humanoids. Probably Cetians, for the machine was
Cetian-made, and they were a smart bunch of devils. They
were the kind that might make a real bid for interstellar
supremacy. The Hainish would be in the conspiracy with
them, of course; all that bleeding-heart stuff in the so-called
directives had a Hainish sound to it. What the long-term
objective of the aliens was, was hard to guess from here;
it probably involved weakening the Terran Government by
tying it up in this "league of worlds" business, until the aliens
were strong enough to make an armed takeover. But their
plan for New Tahiti was easy to see. They'd let the creechies
wipe out the humans for them. Just tie the humans' hands
with a lot of fake "ansible" directives and let the slaughter
begin. Humanoids help humanoids: rats help rats.

And Colonel Dongh had swallowed it. He intended to obey
orders. He had actually said that to Davidson. "I intend to
obey my orders from Terra-HQ, and by God, Don, you'll obey
my orders the same way, and in New Java you'll obey Major
Muhamed's orders there." He was stupid, old Ding Dong, but
he liked Davidson, and Davidson liked him. If it meant be-
traying the human race to an alien conspiracy then he
couldn't obey his orders, but he still felt sorry for the old
soldier. A fool, but a loyal and brave one. Not a born traitor
like that whining, tattling prig Lyubov. If there was one man
he hoped the creechies did get, it was bigdome Raj Lyubov,
the alien-lover.

Some men, especially the asiatiforms and hindi types, are
actually born traitors. Not all, but some. Certain other men
are born saviours. It just happened to be the way they were
made, like being of euraf descent, or like having a good
physique; it wasn't anything he claimed credit for. If he
could save the men and women of New Tahiti, he would; if
he couldn't, he'd make a damn good try; and that was all
there was to it, actually.

The women, now, that rankled. They'd pulled out the 10

Collies who'd been in New Java and none of the new ones were being sent out from Centralville. "Not safe yet," HQ bleated. Pretty rough on the three outpost camps. What did they expect the outposters to do when it was hands off the she-creechies, and all the she-humans were for the lucky bastards at Central? It was going to cause terrific resentment. But it couldn't last long, the whole situation was too crazy to be stable. If they didn't start easing back to normal now the *Shackleton* was gone, then Captain D. Davidson would just have to do a little extra work to get things headed back towards normalcy.

The morning of the day he left Central, they had let loose the whole creechie work-force. Made a big noble speech in pidgin, opened the compound gates, and let out every single tame creechie, carriers, diggers, cooks, dustmen, houseboys, maids, the lot. Not one had stayed. Some of them had been with their masters ever since the start of the colony, four E-years ago. But they had no loyalty. A dog, a chimp would have hung around. These things weren't even that highly developed, they were just about like snakes or rats, just smart enough to turn around and bite you as soon as you let 'em out of the cage. Ding Dong was spla, letting all those creechies loose right in the vicinity. Dumping them on Dump Island and letting them starve would have been actually the best final solution. But Dongh was still panicked by that pair of humanoids and their talky-box. So if the wild creechies on Central were planning to imitate the Smith Camp atrocity, they now had lots of real handy new recruits, who knew the layout of the whole town, the routines, where the arsenal was, where guards were posted, and the rest. If Centralville got burned down, HQ could thank themselves. It would be what they deserved, actually. For letting traitors dupe them, for listening to humanoids and ignoring the advice of men who really knew what the creechies were like.

None of those guys at HQ had come back to camp and found ashes and wreckage and burned bodies, like he had.

And Ok's body, out where they'd slaughtered the logging crew, it had had an arrow sticking out of each eye like some sort of weird insect with antennae sticking out feeling the air, Christ, he kept seeing that.

One thing anyhow, whatever the phoney "directives" said, the boys at Central wouldn't be stuck with trying to use "small side-arms" for self-defence. They had fire throwers and machine guns; the 16 little hoppers had machine guns and were useful for dropping firejelly cans from; the five big hoppers had full armament. But they wouldn't need the big stuff. Just take up a hopper over one of the deforested areas and catch a mess of creechies there, with their damned bows and arrows, and start dropping firejelly cans and watch them run around and burn. It would be all right. It made his belly churn a little to imagine it, just like when he thought about making a woman, or whenever he remembered about when that Sam creechie had attacked him and he had smashed in his whole face with four blows one right after the other. It was eidetic memory plus a more vivid imagination than most men had, no credit due, just happened to be the way he was made.

The fact is, the only time a man is really and entirely a man is when he's just had a woman or just killed another man. That wasn't original, he'd read it in some old books; but it was true. That was why he liked to imagine scenes like that. Even if the creechies weren't actually men.

New Java was the southernmost of the five big lands, just north of the equator, and so was hotter than Central or Smith which were just about perfect climate-wise. Hotter and a lot wetter. It rained all the time in the wet seasons anywhere on New Tahiti, but in the northern lands it was a kind of quiet fine rain that went on and on and never really got you wet or cold. Down here it came in buckets, and there was a monsoon-type storm that you couldn't even walk in, let alone work in. Only a solid roof kept that rain off you, or else the forest. The damn forest was so thick it kept out the storms.

You'd get wet from all the dripping off the leaves, of course, but if you were really inside the forest during one of those monsoons you'd hardly notice the wind was blowing; then you came out in the open and wham! got knocked off your feet by the wind and slobbered all over with the red liquid mud that the rain turned the cleared ground into, and you couldn't duck back into the forest quick enough; and inside the forest it was dark, and hot, and easy to get lost.

Then the C.O., Major Muhamed, was a sticky bastard. Everything at N. J. was done by the book: the logging all in kilo-strips, the fibreweed crap planted in the logged strips, leave to Central granted in strict non-preferential rotation, hallucinogens rationed and their use on duty punished, and so on and so on. However, one good thing about Muhamed was he wasn't always radioing Central. New Java was his camp, and he ran it his way. He didn't like orders from HQ. He obeyed them all right, he'd let the creechies go, and locked up all the guns except little popgun pistols, as soon as the orders came. But he didn't go looking for orders, or for advice. Not from Central or anybody else. He was a self-righteous type: knew he was right. That was his big fault.

When he was on Dongh's staff at HQ Davidson had had occasion sometimes to see the officers' records. His unusual memory held on to such things, and he could recall for instance that Muhamed's IQ was 107. Whereas his own happened to be 118. There was a difference of 11 points; but of course he couldn't say that to old Moo, and Moo couldn't see it, and so there was no way to get him to listen. He thought he knew better than Davidson, and that was that.

They were all a bit sticky at first, actually. None of these men at N. J. knew anything about the Smith Camp atrocity, except that the camp C.O. had left for Central an hour before it happened, and so was the only human that escaped alive. Put like that, it did sound bad. You could see why at first they looked at him like a kind of Jonah, or worse, a kind of Judas even. But when they got to know him they'd know better. They'd begin to see that, far from being a deserter

or traitor, he was dedicated to preventing the colony of
New Tahiti from betrayal. And they'd realise that getting
rid of the creechies was going to be the only way to make this
world safe for the Terran way of life.

It wasn't too hard to start getting that message across to the
loggers. They'd never liked the little green rats, having to
drive them to work all day and guard them all night; but now
they began to understand that the creechies were not only re-
pulsive but dangerous. When Davidson told them what he'd
found at Smith; when he explained how the two humanoids
on the Fleet ship had brainwashed HQ; when he showed them
that wiping out the Terrans on New Tahiti was just a small
part of the whole alien conspiracy against Earth; when he
reminded them of the cold hard figures, twenty-five *hundred*
humans to three *million* creechies—then they began to really
get behind him.

Even the Ecological Control Officer here was with him. Not
like poor old Kees, mad because men shot red deer and then
getting shot in the guts himself by the sneaking creechies.
This fellow, Atranda, was a creechie-hater. Actually he was
kind of spla about them, he had geoshock or something; he
was so afraid the creechies were going to attack the camp
that he acted like some woman afraid of getting raped. But
it was useful to have the local spesh on his side anyhow.

No use trying to line up the C.O.; a good judge of men,
Davidson had seen it was no use almost at once. Muhamed
was rigid-minded. Also he had a prejudice against Davidson
which he wouldn't drop; it had something to do with the
Smith Camp affair. He as much as told Davidson he didn't
consider him a trustworthy officer.

He was a self-righteous bastard, but his running N. J. camp
on such rigid lines was an advantage. A tight organisation,
used to obeying orders, was easier to take over than a loose
one full of independent characters, and easier to keep together as a unit for defensive and offensive miltary operations,
once he was in command. He would have to take command.
Moo was a good logging-camp boss, but no soldier.

Davidson kept busy getting some of the best loggers and junior officers really firmly with him. He didn't hurry. When he had enough of them he could really trust, a squad of ten lifted a few items from old Moo's locked-up room in the Rec House basement full of war toys, and then went off one Sunday into the woods to play.

Davidson had located the creechie town some weeks ago, and had saved up the treat for his men. He could have done it singlehanded, but it was better this way. You got the sense of comradeship, of a real bond among men. They just walked into the place in broad open daylight, and coated all the creechies caught above-ground with firejelly and burned them, then poured kerosene over the warren-roofs and roasted the rest. Those that tried to get out got jellied; that was the artistic part, waiting at the rat-holes for the little rats to come out, letting them think they'd made it, and then just frying them from the feet up so they made torches. That green fur sizzled like crazy.

It actually wasn't much more exciting than hunting real rats, which were about the only wild animals left on Mother Earth, but there was more thrill to it; the creechies were a lot bigger than rats, and you knew they could fight back, though this time they didn't. In fact some of them even lay down instead of running away, just lay there on their backs with their eyes shut. It was sickening. The other fellows thought so too, and one of them actually got sick and vomited after he'd burned up one of the lying-down ones.

Hard up as the men were, they didn't leave even one of the females alive to rape. They had all agreed with Davidson beforehand that it was too damn near perversity. Homosexuality was with other humans, it was normal. These things might be built like human women but they weren't human, and it was better to get your kicks from killing them, and stay *clean*. That had made good sense to all of them, and they stuck to it.

Every one of them kept his trap shut back at camp, no boasting even to their buddies. They were sound men. Not a

word of the expedition got to Muhamed's ears. So far as old
Moo knew, all his men were good little boys just sawing
up logs and keeping away from creechies, yes sir; and he
could go on believing that until D-Day came.

For the creechies would attack. Somewhere. Here, or one
of the camps on King Island, or Central. Davidson knew
that. He was the only officer in the entire colony that did
know it. No credit due, he just happened to know he was
right. Nobody else had believed him, except these men here
whom he'd had time to convince. But the others would all
see, sooner or later, that he was right.

And he was right.

CHAPTER FIVE

It had been a shock, meeting Selver face to face. As he flew back to Central from the foothill village, Lyubov tried to decide why it had been a shock, to analyse out the nerve that had jumped. For after all one isn't usually terrified by a chance meeting with a good friend.

It hadn't been easy to get the headwoman to invite him. Tuntar had been his main locus of study all summer; he had several excellent informants there and was on good terms with the Lodge and with the headwoman, who had let him observe and participate in the community freely. Wangling an actual invitation out of her, via some of the ex-serfs still in the area, had taken a long time, but at last she had complied, giving him, according to the new directives, a genuine "occasion arranged by the Athsheans". His own conscience, rather than the Colonel, had insisted on this. Dongh wanted him to go. He was worried about the Creechie Threat. He told Lyubov to size them up, to "see how they're reacting now that we're leaving them strictly alone". He hoped for reassurance. Lyubov couldn't decide whether the report he'd be turning it would reassure Colonel Dongh, or not.

For ten miles out of Central, the plain had been logged and the stumps had all rotted away; it was now a great dull flat of fibreweed, hairy grey in the rain. Under those hirsute leaves the seedling shrubs got their first growth, the sumacs, dwarf aspens, and salviforms which, grown, would in turn protect the seedling trees. Left alone, in this even, rainy climate, this area might reforest itself within thirty years and reattain the full climax forest within a hundred. Left alone.

Suddenly the forest began again, in space not time: under the helicopter the infinitely various green of leaves covered the slow swells and foldings of the hills of North Sornol.

Like most Terrans on Terra, Lyubov had never walked among wild trees at all, never seen a wood larger than a city block. At first on Athshe he had felt oppressed and uneasy in the forest, stifled by its endless crowd and incoherence of trunks, branches, leaves in the perpetual greenish or brownish twilight. The mass and jumble of various competitive lives all pushing and swelling outwards and upwards towards light, the silence made up of many little meaningless noises, the total vegetable indifference to the presence of mind, all this had troubled him, and like the others he had kept to clearings and to the beach. But little by little he had begun to like it. Gosse teased him, calling him Mr Gibbon; in fact Lyubov looked rather like a gibbon, with a round, dark face, long arms, and hair greying early; but gibbons were extinct. Like it or not, as a hilfer he had to go into the forests to find the hilfs; and now after four years of it he was completely at home under the trees, more so perhaps than anywhere else.

He had also come to like the Athsheans' names for their own lands and places, sonorous two-syllabled words: Sornol, Tuntar, Eshreth, Eshsen—that was now Centralville—Endtor, Abtan, and above all Athshe, which meant the Forest, and the World. So earth, terra, tellus mean both the soil and the planet, two meanings and one. But to the Athsheans soil, ground, earth was not that to which the dead return and by which the living live: the substance of their world was not earth, but forest. Terran man was clay, red dust. Athshean man was branch and root. They did not carve figures of themselves in stone, only in wood.

He brought the hopper down in a small glade north of the town, and walked in past the Women's Lodge. The smell of an Athshean settlement hung pungent in the air, woodsmoke, dead fish, aromatic herbs, alien sweat. The atmosphere of an underground house, if a Terran could fit himself in at all, was a rare compound of CO_2 and stinks. Lyubov had spent many intellectually stimulating hours doubled up and suffocating in the reeking gloom of the Men's Lodge in Tuntar. But it didn't look as if he would be invited in this time.

Of course the townsfolk knew of the Smith Camp massacre, now six weeks ago. They would have known of it soon, for word got around fast among the islands, though not so fast as to constitute a "mysterious power of telepathy" as the loggers liked to believe. The townsfolk also knew that the 1200 slaves at Centralville had been freed soon after the Smith Camp massacre, and Lyubov agreed with the Colonel that the natives might take the second event to be a result of the first. That gave what Colonel Dongh would call "an erroneous impression", but it probably wasn't important. What was important was that the slaves had been freed. Wrongs done could not be righted, but at least they were not still being done. They could start over: the natives without that painful, unanswerable wonder as to why the "yumens" treated men like animals; and he without the burden of explanation and the gnawing of irremediable guilt.

Knowing how they valued candour and direct speech concerning frightening or troublous matters, he expected that people in Tuntar would talk about these things with him, in triumph, or apology, or rejoicing, or puzzlement. No one did. No one said much of anything to him.

He had come in late afternoon, which was like arriving in a Terran city just after dawn. Athsheans did sleep—the colonists' opinion, as often, ignored observable fact—but their physiological low was between noon and four p.m., whereas with Terrans it is usually between two and five a.m.; and they had a double-peak cycle of high temperature and high activity, coming in the two twilights, dawn and evening. Most adults slept five or six hours in 24, in several catnaps; and adept men slept as little as two hours in 24; so if one discounted both their naps and their dreaming-states as "laziness", one might say they never slept. It was much easier to say that than to understand what they actually did do— At this point, in Tuntar, things were just beginning to stir again after the late-day slump.

Lyubov noticed a good many strangers. They looked at him, but none approached; they were mere presences passing on other paths in the dusk of the great oaks. At last someone he knew came along his path, the headwoman's cousin Sherrar, an old woman of small importance and small understanding. She greeted him civilly, but did not or would not respond to his inquiries about the headwoman and his two best informants, Egath the orchard-keeper and Tubab the Dreamer. Oh, the headwoman was very busy, and who was Egath, did he mean Geban, and Tubab might be here or perhaps he was there, or not. She stuck to Lyubov, and nobody else spoke to him. He worked his way, accompanied by the hobbling, complaining, tiny, green crone, across the groves and glades of Tuntar to the Men's Lodge. "They're busy in there," said Sherrar.

"Dreaming?"

"However should I know? Come along now, Lyubov, come see. . . ." She knew he always wanted to see things, but she couldn't think what to show him to draw him away. "Come see the fishing-nets," she said feebly.

A girl passing by, one of the Young Hunters, looked up at him: a black look, a stare of animosity such as he had never received from any Athshean, unless perhaps from a little child frightened into scowling by his height and his hairless face. But this girl was not frightened.

"All right," he said to Sherrar, feeling that his only course was docility. If the Athsheans had indeed developed—at last, and abruptly—the sense of group enmity, then he must accept this, and simply try to show them that he remained a reliable, unchanging friend.

But how could their way of feeling and thinking have changed so fast, after so long? And why? At Smith Camp, provocation had been immediate and intolerable: Davidson's cruelty would drive even Athsheans to violence. But this town, Tuntar, had never been attacked by the Terrans, had suffered no slave-raids, had not seen the local forest logged or burned. He, Lyubov himself, had been there—the anthropologist cannot always leave his own shadow out of the picture he draws—but not for over two months now. They had got the news from Smith, and there were among them now refugees, ex-slaves, who had suffered at the Terrans' hands and would talk about it. But would news and hearsay change the hearers, change them radically?—when their unaggressiveness ran so deep in them, right through their culture and society and on down into their subconscious, their "dream time", and perhaps into their very physiology? That an Athshean could be provoked, by atrocious cruelty, to attempt murder, he knew: he had seen it happen—once. That a disrupted community might be similarly provoked by similarly intolerable injuries, he had to believe: it had happened at Smith Camp. But that talk and hearsay, no matter how frightening and outrageous, could enrage a settled community of these people to the point where they acted against their customs and reason, broke entirely out of their whole style of living, this he couldn't believe. It was psychologically improbable. Some element was missing.

Old Tubab came out of the Lodge, just as Lyubov passed in front of it. Behind the old man came Selver.

Selver crawled out of the tunnel-door, stood upright, blinked at the rain-greyed, foliage-dimmed brightness of daylight. His dark eyes met Lyubov's, looking up. Neither spoke. Lyubov was badly frightened.

Flying home in the hopper, analysing out the shocked nerve, he thought, why fear? Why was I afraid of Selver? Unprovable intuition or mere false analogy? Irrational in any case.

Nothing between Selver and Lyubov had changed. What Selver had done at Smith Camp could be justified; even if it couldn't be justified, it made no difference. The friendship between them was too deep to be touched by moral doubt. They had worked very hard together; they had taught each other, in rather more than the literal sense, their languages.

They had spoken without reserve. And Lyubov's love for his friend was deepened by that gratitude the saviour feels towards the one whose life he has been privileged to save.

Indeed he had scarcely realised until that moment how deep his liking and loyalty to Selver were. Had his fear in fact been the personal fear that Selver might, having learned racial hatred, reject him, despise his loyalty, and treat him not as "you", but as "one of them"?

After that long first gaze Selver came forward slowly and greeted Lyubov, holding out his hands.

Touch was a main channel of communication among the forest people. Among Terrans touch is always likely to imply threat, aggression, and so for them there is often nothing between the formal handshake and the sexual caress. All that black was filled by the Athsheans with varied customs of touch. Caress as signal and reassurance was as essential to them as it is to mother and child or to lover and lover; but its significance was social, not only maternal and sexual. It was part of their language. It was therefore patterned, codified, yet infinitely modifiable. "They're always pawing each other," some of the colonists sneered, unable to see in these touch-exchanges anything but their own eroticism which, forced to concentrate itself exclusively on sex and then repressed and frustrated, invades and poisons every sensual pleasure, every humane response: the victory of a blinded, furtive Cupid over the great brooding mother of all the seas and stars, all the leaves of trees, all the gestures of men, Venus Genetrix....

So Selver came forward with his hands held out, shook Lyubov's hand Terran fashion, and then took both his arms with a stroking motion just above the elbow. He was not much more than half Lyubov's height, which made all gestures difficult and ungainly for both of them, but there was nothing uncertain or childlike in the touch of his small, thin-boned, green-furred hand on Lyubov's arms. It was a reassurance. Lyubov was very glad to get it.

"Selver, what luck to meet you here. I want very much to talk with you—"

"I can't, now, Lyubov."

He spoke gently, but when he spoke Lyubov's hope of an unaltered friendship vanished. Selver had changed. He was changed, radically: from the root.

"Can I come back," Lyubov said urgently, "another day, and talk with you, Selver? It is important to me—"

"I leave here today," Selver said even more gently, but letting go Lyubov's arms, and also looking away. He thus put himself literally out of touch. Civility required that Lyubov do the same, and let the conversation end. But then there would be no one to talk to. Old Tubab had not even looked at him; the town had turned its back on him. And this was Selver, who had been his friend.

"Selver, this killing at Kelme Deva, maybe you think that lies between us. But it does not. Maybe it brings us closer together. And your people in the slave-pens, they've all been set free, so that wrong no longer lies between us. And even if it does—it always did—all the same I ... I am the same man I was, Selver."

At first the Athshean made no response. His strange face, the large deep-set eyes, the strong features misshapen by scars and blurred by the short silken fur that followed and yet obscured all contours, this face turned from Lyubov, shut, obstinate. Then suddenly he looked round as if against his own intent. "Lyubov, you shouldn't have come here. You should leave Central two nights from now. I don't know what you are. It would be better if I had never known you."

And with that he was off, a light walk like a long-legged cat, a green flicker among the dark oaks of Tuntar, gone. Tubab followed slowly after him, still without a glance at Lyubov. A fine rain fell without sound on the oak-leaves and on the narrow pathways to the Lodge and the river. Only if you listened intently could you hear the rain, too multitudinous a music for one mind to grasp, a single endless chord played on the entire forest.

"Selver is a god," said old Sherrar. "Come and see the fishing nets now."

Lyubov declined. It would be impolite and impolitic to stay; anyway he had no heart to.

He tried to tell himself that Selver had not been rejecting him, Lyubov, but him as a Terran. It made no difference. It never does.

He was always disagreeably surprised to find how vulnerable his feelings were, how much it hurt him to be hurt. This sort of adolescent sensitivity was shameful, he should have a tougher hide by now.

The little crone, her green fur all dusted and besilvered with raindrops, sighed with relief when he said goodbye. As he started the hopper he had to grin at the sight of her, hop-hobbling off into the trees as fast as she could go, like a little toad that has escaped a snake.

Quality is an important matter, but so is quantity: relative size. The normal adult reaction to a very much smaller person may be arrogant, or protective, or patronising, or affectionate, or bullying, but whatever it is it's liable to be better fitted to a child than to an adult. Then, when the child-sized person was furry, a further response got called upon, which Lyubov had labelled the Teddybear Reaction. Since the Athsheans used caress so much, its manifestation was not inappropriate, but its motivation remained suspect. And finally there was the inevitable Freak Reaction, the flinching away from what is human but does not quite look so.

But quite outside of all that was the fact that the Athsheans, like Terrans, were simply funny-looking at times. Some of them did look like little toads, owls, caterpillars. Sherrar was not the first little old lady who had struck Lyubov as looking funny from behind. . . .

And that's one trouble with the colony, he thought as he lifted the hopper and Tuntar vanished beneath the oaks and the leafless orchards. We haven't got any old women. No old men either, except Dongh and he's only about sixty. But old women are different from everybody else, they say what they think. The Athsheans are governed, in so far as they have government, by old women. Intellect to the men, politics to the women, and ethics to the interaction of both: that's their arrangement. It has charm, and it works—for them. I wish the Administration had sent out a couple of grannies along with all those nubile fertile high-breasted young women. Now that girl I had over the other night, she's really very nice, and nice in bed, she has a kind heart, but my God it'll be forty years before she'll say anything to a man....

But all the time, beneath his thoughts concerning old women and young ones, the shock persisted, the intuition or recognition that would not let itself be recognised.

He must think this out before he reported to HQ.

Selver: what about Selver, then?

Selver was certainly a key figure to Lyubov. Why? Because he knew him well, or because of some actual power in his personality, which Lyubov had never consciously appreciated?

But he had appreciated it; he had picked Selver out very soon as an extraordinary person. "Sam", he had been then, bodyservant for three officers sharing a prefab. Lyubov remembered Benson boasting what a good creechie they'd got, they'd broke him in right.

Many Athsheans, especially Dreamers from the Lodges, could not change their polycyclic sleep-pattern to fit the Terran one. If they caught up with their normal sleep at night, that prevented them from catching up with the REM or paradoxical sleep, whose 120-minute cycle ruled their life both day and night, and could not be fitted in to the Terran workday. Once you have learned to do your dreaming wide awake, to balance your sanity not on the razor's edge of reason but on the double support, the fine balance, of reason and dream, once you have learned that, you cannot unlearn it any more than you can unlearn to think. So many of the men became groggy, confused, withdrawn, even catatonic. Women, bewildered and abased, behaved with the sullen listlessness of the newly enslaved. Male non-adepts and some of the younger Dreamers did best; they adapted, working hard in the logging camps or becoming clever servants. Sam had been one of these, an efficient, characterless body-servant, cook, laundry-boy, butler, backsoaper and scapegoat for his three masters. He had learned how to be invisible. Lyubov borrowed him as an ethnological informant, and had, by some affinity of mind and nature, won Sam's trust at once. He found Sam the ideal informant, trained in his people's customs, perceptive of their significances, and quick to trans-late them, to make them intelligible to Lyubov, bridging the gap between two languages, two cultures, two species of the genus Man.

For two years Lyubov had been travelling, studying, inter-viewing, observing, and had failed to get at the key that would let him into the Athshean mind. He didn't even know where the lock was. He had studied the Athsheans' sleeping-habits and found that they apparently had no sleeping-habits. He had wired countless electrodes onto countless furry green skulls, and failed to make any sense at all out of the familiar patterns, the spindles and jags, the alphas and deltas and thetas, that appeared on the graph. It was Selver who had made him understand, at last, the Athshean signifi-cance of the word "dream", which was also the word for "root", and so hand him the key of the kingdom of the forest people. It was with Selver as EEG subject that he had first seen with comprehension the extraordinary impulse-patterns of a brain entering a dreamstate neither sleeping nor awake : a condition which related to Terran dreaming-sleep as the Parthenon to a mud hut: the same thing basically, but with the addition of complexity, quality, and control.

What then, what more?

Selver might have escaped. He stayed, first as a valet, then (through one of Lyubov's few useful perquisites as a Spesh) as Scientific Aide, still locked up nightly with all other creechies in the pen (the Voluntary Autochthonous Labour Personnel Quarters). "I'll fly you up to Tuntar and work with you there," Lyubov had said, about the third time he talked with Selver, "for God's sake why stay here?"—"My wife Thele is in the pen," Selver had said. Lyubov had tried to get her released, but she was in the HQ kitchen, and the sergeants who managed the kitchen-gang resented any interference from "brass" and "speshes". Lyubov had to be very careful, lest they take out their resentment on the woman. She and Selver had both seemed willing to wait patiently until both could escape or be freed. Male and female creechies were strictly segregated in the pens—why, no one seemed to know—and husband and wife rarely saw each other. Lyubov managed to arrange meetings for them in his hut, which he had to himself at the north end of town. It was when Thele was returning to HQ from one such meeting that Davidson had seen her and apparently been struck by her frail, frightened grace. He had had her brought to his quarters that night, and had raped her.

He had killed her in the act, perhaps; this had happened before, a result of the physical disparity; or else she had stopped living. Like some Terrans the Athsheans had the knack of the authentic death-wish, and could cease to live. In either case it was Davidson who had killed her. Such murders had occurred before. What had not occurred before was what Selver did, the second day after her death.

Lyubov had got there only at the end. He could recall the sounds; himself running down Main Street in hot sunlight; the dust, the knot of men. The whole thing could have lasted only five minutes, a long time for a homicidal fight. When Lyubov got there Selver was blinded with blood, a sort of toy for Davidson to play with, and yet he had picked himself up and was coming back, not with berserk rage but with intelligent despair. He kept coming back. It was Davidson who was scared into rage at last by that terrible persistence; knocking Selver down with a side-blow he had moved forward lifting his booted foot to stamp on the skull. Even as he moved, Lyubov had broken into the circle. He stopped the fight (for whatever blood-thirst the ten or twelve men

watching had had, was more than appeased, and they backed
Lyubov when he told Davidson hands off); and thenceforth
he hated Davidson, and was hated by him, having come between the killer and his death.

For if it's all the rest of us who are killed by the suicide,
it's himself whom the murderer kills; only he has to do it
over, and over, and over.

Lyubov had picked up Selver, a light weight in his arms.
The mutilated face had pressed against his shirt so that the
blood soaked through against his own skin. He had taken
Selver to his own bungalow, splinted his broken wrist, done
what he could for his face, kept him in his own bed, night
after night tried to talk to him, to reach him in the desolation
of his grief and shame. It was, of course, against regulations.

Nobody mentioned the regulations to him. They did not
have to. He knew he was forfeiting most of what favour he
had ever had with the officers of the colony.

He had been careful to keep on the right side of HQ,
objecting only to extreme cases of brutality against the
natives, using persuasion not defiance, and conserving what
shred of power and influence he had. He could not prevent
the exploitation of the Athsheans. It was much worse than
his training had led him to expect, but he could do little
about it here and now. His reports to the Administration and the Committee on Rights might—after the roundtrip
of 54 years—have some effect; Terra might even decide that
the Open Colony policy for Athshe was a bad mistake. Better
54 years late than never. If he lost the tolerance of his superiors
here they would censor or invalidate his reports, and there
would be no hope at all.

But he was too angry now to keep up his strategy. To
hell with the others, if they insisted on seeing his care of a
friend as an insult to Mother Earth and a betrayal of
the colony. If they labelled him "creechie-lover" his useful-
ness to the Athsheans would be impaired; but he could not
set a possible, general good above Selver's imperative need.
You can't save a people by selling your friend. Davidson,

curiously infuriated by the minor injuries Selver had done him and by Lyubov's interference, had gone around saying he intended to finish off that rebel creechie; he certainly would do so if he got the chance. Lyubov stayed with Selver night and day for two weeks, and then flew him out of Central and put him down in a west coast town, Broter, where he had no relatives.

There was no penalty for aiding slaves to escape, since the Athsheans were not slaves at all except in fact: they were Voluntary Autochthonous Labour Personnel. Lyubov was not even reprimanded. But the regular officers distrusted him totally, instead of partially, from then on; and even his colleagues in the Special Services, the exobiologist, the ag and forestry coordinators, the ecologists, variously let him know that he had been irrational, quixotic, or stupid. "Did you think you were coming on a picnic?" Gosse had demanded.

"No. I didn't think it would be any bloody picnic," Lyubov answered, morose.

"I can't see why any hilfer voluntarily ties himself up to an Open Colony. You know the people you're studying are going to get ploughed under, and probably wiped out. It's the way things are. It's human nature, and you must know you can't change that. Then why come and watch the process? Masochism?"

"I don't know what 'human nature' is. Maybe leaving descriptions of what we wipe out is part of human nature— Is it much pleasanter for an ecologist, really?"

Gosse ignored this. "All right then, write up your descriptions. But keep out of the carnage. A biologist studying a rat colony doesn't start reaching in and rescuing pet rats of his that get attacked, you know."

At this Lyubov had blown loose. He had taken too much. "No, of course not," he said. "A rat can be a pet, but not a friend. Selver is my friend. In fact he's the only man on this world whom I consider to be a friend." That had hurt poor old Gosse, who wanted to be a father-figure to Lyubov, and it had done nobody any good. Yet it had been true. And the truth shall make you free.... I like Selver, respect him; saved him; suffered with him; fear him. Selver is my friend.

Selver is a god.

So the little green crone had said as if everybody knew it, as flatly as she might have said So-and-so is a hunter. "Selver sha'ab." What did *sha'ab* mean, though? Many words of the Women's Tongue, the everyday speech of the Athsheans, came from the Men's Tongue that was the same in all communities, and these words often were not only two-syllabled but two-sided. They were coins, obverse and reverse. *Sha'ab* meant god, or numinous entity, or powerful being; it also meant something quite different, but Lyubov could not remember what. By this stage in his thinking, he was home in his bungalow, and had only to look it up in the dictionary which he and Selver had compiled in four months of exhausting but harmonious work. Of course: *sha'ab*, translator.

It was almost too pat, too apposite.

Were the two meanings connected? Often they were, yet not so often as to constitute a rule. If a god was a translator, what did he translate? Selver was indeed a gifted interpreter, but that gift had found expression only through the fortuity of a truly foreign language having been brought into his world. Was a *sha'ab* one who translated the language of dream and philosophy, the Men's Tongue, into the everyday speech? But all Dreamers could do that. Might he then be one who could translate into waking life the central experience of vision: one serving as a link between the two realities, considered by the Athsheans as equal, the dream-time and the world-time, whose connections, though vital, are obscure. A link: one who could speak aloud the perceptions of the subconscious. To "speak" that tongue is to act. To do a new thing. To change or to be changed, radically, from the root. For the root is the dream.

And the translator is the god. Selver had brought a new word into the language of his people. He had done a new deed. The word, the deed, murder. Only a god could lead so great a newcomer as Death across the bridge between the worlds.

But had he learned to kill his fellowmen among his own dreams of outrage and bereavement, or from the undreamed-of actions of the strangers? Was he speaking his own language, or was he speaking Captain Davidson's? That which seemed to rise from the root of his own suffering and express his own changed being, might in fact be an infection, a foreign plague, which would not make a new people of his race, but would destroy them.

It was not in Raj Lyubov's nature to think, "What can I do?" Character and training disposed him not to interfere in other men's business. His job was to find out what they did, and his inclination was to let them go on doing it. He preferred to be enlightened, rather than to enlighten; to seek facts rather than the Truth. But even the most unmissionary soul, unless he pretends he has no emotions, is sometimes faced with a choice between commission and omission. "What are they doing?" abruptly becomes, "What are we doing?" and then, "What must I do?"

That he had reached such a point of choice now, he knew, and yet did not know clearly why, nor what alternatives were offered him.

He could do no more to improve the Athsheans' chance of survival at the moment; Lepennon, Or, and the ansible had done more than he had hoped to see done in his lifetime. The Administration on Terra was explicit in every ansible communication, and Colonel Dongh, though under pressure from some of his staff and logging bosses to ignore the directives, was carrying out orders. He was a loyal officer; and besides, the *Shackleton* would be coming back to observe and report on how orders were being carried out. Reports home meant something, now that this ansible, this *machina ex machina*, functioned to prevent all the comfortable old colonial autonomy, and make you answerable within your own lifetime for what you did. There was no more 54-year margin for error. Policy was no longer static. A decision by the League of Worlds might now lead overnight to the colony's being limited to one Land, or forbidden to cut trees, or encouraged to kill natives—no telling. How the League worked and what sort of policies it was developing could not yet be guessed from the flat directives of the Administration. Dongh was worred by these multiple-choice futures, but Lyubov enjoyed them. In diversity is life and where there's life there's hope, was the general sum of his creed, a modest one to be sure.

The colonists were letting the Athsheans alone and they were letting the colonists alone. A healthy situation, and one not to be disturbed unnecessarily. The only thing likely to disturb it was fear.

At the moment the Athsheans might be expected to be suspicious and still resentful, but not particularly afraid. As for the panic felt in Centralville at news of the Smith Camp massacre, nothing had happened to revive it. No Athshean anywhere had shown any violence since; and with the slaves gone, the creechies all vanished back into their forests, there was no more constant irritation of xenophobia. The colonists were at last beginning to relax.

If Lyubov reported that he had seen Selver at Tuntar, Dongh and the others would be alarmed. They might insist on trying to capture Selver and bring him in for trial. The Colonial Code forbade prosecution of a member of one planetary society under the laws of another, but the Court Martial over-rode such distinctions. They could try, convict, and shoot Selver. With Davidson brought back from New Java to give evidence. Oh no, Lyubov thought, shoving the dictionary onto an overcrowded shelf. Oh no, he thought, and thought no more about it. So he made his choice without even knowing he had made one.

He turned in a brief report next day. It said that Tuntar was going about its business as usual, and that he had not been turned away or threatened. It was a soothing report, and the most inaccurate one Lyubov ever wrote. It omitted everything of significance: the headwoman's non-appearance, Tubab's refusal to greet Lyubov, the large number of strangers in town, the young huntress' expression, Selver's presence... Of course that last was an intentional omission, but otherwise the report was quite factual, he thought; he had merely omitted subjective impressions, as a scientist should. He had a severe migrane whilst writing the report, and a worse one after submitting it.

He dreamed a lot that night, but could not remember his dreams in the morning. Late in the second night after his visit to Tuntar he woke, and in the hysterical whooping of the alarm-siren and the thudding of explosions he faced, at last, what he had refused. He was the only man in Central-ville not taken by surprise. In that moment he knew what he was: a traitor.

And yet even now it was not clear in his mind that this was an Athshean raid. It was the terror in the night.

His own hut had been ignored, standing in its yard away from other houses; perhaps the trees around it protected it, he thought as he hurried out. The centre of town was all on fire. Even the stone cube of HQ burned from within like a broken kiln. The ansible was in there: the precious link. There were fires also in the direction of the helicopter port and the Field. Where had they got explosives? How had the fires got going all at once? All the buildings along both sides of Main Street, built of wood, were burning, the sound of the burning was terrible. Lyubov ran towards the fires. Water flooded the way; he thought at first it was from a fire-hose, then realised the main from the river Menend was flooding uselessly over the ground while the houses burned with that hideous sucking roar. How had they done this? There were guards, there were always guards in jeeps at the Field. . . . Shots: volleys, the yatter of a machine gun. All around Lyubov were small running figures, but he ran among them without giving them much thought. He was abreast of the Hostel now, and saw a girl standing in the doorway, fire flicker-ing at her back and a clear escape before her. She did not move. He shouted at her, then ran across the yard to her and wrested her hands free of the doorjambs which she clung to in panic, pulling her away by force, saying gently, "Come on, honey, come on." She came then, but not quite soon enough. As they crossed the yard the front of the upper storey, blazing from within, fell slowly forward, pushed by the timbers of the collapsing roof. Shingles and beams shot out like shell-fragments; a blazing beam-end struck Lyubov and knocked him sprawling. He lay face down in the firelit lake of mud. He did not see a little green-furred huntress leap at the girl, drag her down backwards, and cut her throat. He did not see anything.

CHAPTER SIX

No songs were sung that night. There was only shouting and silence. When the flying ships burned Selver exulted, and tears came into his eyes, but no words into his mouth. He turned away in silence, the fire thrower heavy in his arms, to lead his group back into the city.

Each group of people from the West and North was led by an ex-slave like himself, one who had served the yumens in Central and knew the buildings and ways of the city.

Most of the people who came to the attack that night had never seen the yumen city; many of them had never seen a yumen. They had come because they followed Selver, because they were driven by the evil dream and only Selver could teach them how to master it. There were hundreds and hundreds of them, men and women; they had waited in utter silence in the rainy darkness all around the edges of the city, while the ex-slaves, two or three at a time, did those things which they judged must be done first: break the water-pipe, cut the wires that carried light from Generator House, break into and rob the Arsenal. The first deaths, those of guards, had been silent, accomplished with hunting weapons, noose, knife, arrow, very quickly, in the dark. The dynamite, stolen earlier in the night from the logging camp ten miles south, was prepared in the Arsenal, the basement of HQ Building, while fires were set in other places; and then the alarm went off and the fires blazed and both night and silence fled. Most of the thunderclap and tree-fall crashing of gunfire came from the yumens defending themselves, for only ex-slaves had taken weapons from the Arsenal and used them; all the rest kept to their own lances, knives, and bows. But it was the dynamite, placed and ignited by Reswan and others who had worked in the loggers' slave-pen, that made the noise that conquered all other noises, and blew out the walls of the HQ Building and destroyed the hangars and the ships.

There were about seventeen hundred yumens in the city that night, about five hundred of them female; all the yumen females were said to be there now, that was why Selver and the others had decided to act, though not all the people who wished to come had yet gathered. Between four and five thousand men and women had come through the forests to the Meeting at Endtor, and from there to this place, to this night.

The fires burned huge, and the smell of burning and of butchering was foul.

Selver's mouth was dry and his throat sore, so that he could not speak, and longed for water to drink. As he led his group down the middle path of the city, a yumen came running towards him, looming huge in the black and dazzle of the smoky air. Selver lifted the fire thrower and pulled back on the tongue of it, even as the yumen slipped in mud and fell scrambling to its knees. No hissing jet of flame sprang from the machine, it had all been spent on burning the airships that had not been in the hangar. Selver dropped the heavy machine. The yumen was not armed, and was male. Selver tried to say, "Let him run away," but his voice was weak, and two men, hunters of the Abtam Glades, had leapt past him even as he spoke, holding their long knives up. The big naked hands clutched at air, and dropped limp. The big corpse lay in a heap on the path. There were many others lying dead, there in what had been the centre of the city. There was not much noise any more except the noise of the fires.

Selver parted his lips and hoarsely sent up the home-call that ends the hunt; those with him took it up more clearly and loudly, in carrying falsetto; other voices answered it, near and far off in the mist and reek and flame-shot darkness of the night. Instead of leading his group at once from the city, he signalled them to go on, and himself went aside, onto the muddy ground between the path and a building which had burned and fallen. He stepped across a dead female yumen and bent over one that lay pinned down under a great, charred beam of wood. He could not see the features obliterated by mud and shadow.

It was not just; it was not necessary; he need not have looked at that one among so many dead. He need not have known him in the dark. He started to go after his group. Then he turned back; straining, lifted the beam off Lyubov's back; knelt down, slipping one hand under the heavy head so that Lyubov seemed to lie easier, his face clear of the earth; and so knelt there, motionless.

He had not slept for four days and had not been still to dream for longer than that—he did not know how long. He had acted, spoken, travelled, planned, night and day, ever since he left Broter with his followers from Cadast. He had gone from city to city speaking to the people of the forest, telling them the new thing, waking them from the dream into the world, arranging the thing done this night, talking, always talking and hearing others talk, never in silence and never alone. They had listened, they had heard and had come to follow him, to follow the new path. They had taken up the fire they feared into their own hands : taken up the mastery over the evil dream : and loosed the death they feared upon their enemy. All had been done as he said it should be done. All had gone as he said it would go. The lodges and many dwellings of the yumens were burnt, their airships burnt or broken, their weapons stolen or destroyed : and their females were dead. The fires were burning out, the night growing very dark, fouled with smoke. Selver could scarcely see; he looked up to the east, wondering if it were nearing dawn. Kneeling there in the mud among the dead he thought, This is the dream now, the evil dream. I thought to drive it, but it drives me.

In the dream, Lyubov's lips moved a little against the

palm of his own hand; Selver looked down and saw the dead
man's eyes open. The glare of dying fires shone on the sur-
face of them. After a while he spoke Selver's name.

"Lyubov, why did you stay here? I told you to be out of
the city this night." So Selver spoke in dream, harthly, as if
he were angry at Lyubov.

"Are you the prisoner?" Lyubov said, faintly and not
lifting his head, but in so commonplace a voice that Selver
knew for a moment that this was not the dream-time but
the world-time, the forest's night. "Or am I?"

"Neither, both, how do I know? All the engines and
machines are burned, All the women are dead. We let the
men run away if they would. I told them not to set fire to
your house, the books will be all right. Lyubov, why aren't
you like the others?"

"I am like them. A man. Like them. Like you."

"No. You are different—"

"I am like them. And so are you. Listen, Selver. Don't
go on. You must not go on killing other men. You must go
back ... to your own ... to your roots."

"When your people are gone, then the evil dream will
stop."

"Now," Lyubov said, trying to lift his head, but his back
was broken. He looked up at Selver and opened his mouth
to speak. His gaze dropped away and looked into the other
time, and his lips remained parted, unspeaking. His breath
whistled a little in his throat.

They were calling Selver's name, many voices far away,
calling over and over. "I can't stay with you, Lyubov!"
Selver said in tears, and when there was no answer stood
up and tried to run away. But in the dream-darkness he
could go only very slowly, like one wading through deep water.
The Ash Spirit walked in front of him, taller than Lyubov
or any yumen, tall as a tree, not turning its white mask to
him. As Selver went he spoke to Lyubov: "We'll go back,"
he said. "I will go back. Now. We will go back, now, I promise you, Lyubov!"

But his friend, the gentle one, who had saved his life and betrayed his dream, Lyubov did not reply. He walked somewhere in the night near Selver, unseen, and quiet as death.

A group of the people of Tuntar came on Selver wandering in the dark, weeping and speaking, overmastered by dream; they took him with them in their swift return to Endtor.

In the makeshift Lodge there, a tent on the river-bank, he lay helpless and insane for two days and nights, while the Old Men tended him. All that time people kept coming in to Endtor and going out again, returning to the Place of Eshsen which had been called Central, burying their dead there and the alien dead: of theirs more than three hundred, of the others more than seven hundred. There were about five hundred yumens locked into the compound, the creechie-pens, which, standing empty and apart, had not been burnt. As many more had escaped, some of whom had got to the logging camps farther south, which had not been attacked; those who were still hiding and wandering in the forest or the Cut Lands were hunted down. Some were killed, for many of the younger hunters and huntresses still heard only Selver's voice saying *Kill them*. Others had left the night of killing behind them as if it had been a nightmare, the evil dream that must be understood lest it be repeated; and these, faced with a thirsty, exhausted yumen cowering in a thicket, could not kill him. So maybe he killed them. There were groups of ten and twenty yumens, armed with logger's axes and hand-guns, though few had ammunition left; these groups were tracked until sufficient numbers were hidden in the forest about them, then overpowered, bound, and led back to Eshsen. They were all captured within two or three days, for all that part of Sornol was swarming with the people of the forest, there had never in the knowledge of any man been half or a tenth so great a gathering of people in one place; some still coming in from distant towns and other Lands, others already going home again. The captured yumens were put in among the others in the compound, though it was overcrowded and the huts were too small for yumens. They were watered, fed twice daily, and guarded by a couple of hundred armed hunters at all times.

In the afternoon following the Night of Eshsen an airship came rattling out of the east and flew low as if to land, then shot upward like a bird of prey that misses its kill, and circled the wrecked landing-place, the smouldering city, and the Cut Lands. Reswan had seen to it that the radios were destroyed, and perhaps it was the silence of the radios that had brought the airship from Kushil or Rieshwel, where there were three small towns of yumens. The prisoners in the compound rushed out of the barracks and yelled at the machine whenever it came rattling overhead, and once it dropped an object on a small parachute into the compound: at last it rattled off into the sky.

There were four such winged ships left on Athshe now, three on Kushil and one on Rieshwel, all of the small kind that carried four men; they also carried machine guns and flamethrowers, and they weighed much on the minds of Reswan and the others, while Selver lay lost to them, walking the cryptic ways of the other time.

He woke into the world-time on the third day, thin, dazed, hungry, silent. After he had bathed in the river and had eaten, he listened to Reswan and the headwoman of Berre and the others chosen as leaders. They told him how the world had gone while he dreamed. When he had heard them all, he looked about at them and they saw the god in him. In the sickness of disgust and fear that followed the Night of Eshsen, some of them had come to doubt. Their dreams were uneasy and full of blood and fire; they were surrounded all day by strangers, people come from all over the forests, hundreds of them, thousands, all gathered here like kites to carrion, none knowing another: and it seemed to them as if the end of things had come and nothing would ever be the same, or be right, again. But in Selver's presence they remembered purpose; their distress was quietened, and they waited for him to speak.

"The killing is all done," he said. "Make sure that everyone knows that." He looked round at them. "I have to talk with the ones in the compound. Who is leading them in there?"

"Turkey, Flapfeet, Weteyes," said Reswan, the ex-slave.

"Turkey's alive? Good. Help me get up, Greda. I have eels for bones. . . ."

When he had been afoot a while he was stronger, and within the hour he set off for Eshsen, two hours' walk from Endtor.

When they came Reswan mounted a ladder set against the compound wall and bawled in the pidgin-English taught the slaves, "Dong-a come to gate hurry-up-quick!"

Down in the alleys between the squat cement barracks, some of the yumens yelled and threw clods of dirt at him. He ducked, and waited.

The old Colonel did not come out, but Gosse, whom they called Weteyes, came limping out of a hut and called up to Reswan, "Colonel Dongh is ill, he cannot come out."

"Ill what kind?"

"Bowels, water-illness. What you want?"

"Talk-talk— My lord god," Reswan said in his own language, looking down at Selver, "the Turkey's hiding, do you want to talk with Weteyes?"

"All right."

"Watch the gate there, you bowmen!— To gate, Mis-ter Goss-a, hurry-up-quick!"

The gate was opened just wide enough and long enough for Gosse to squeeze out. He stood in front of it alone, facing the group led by Selver. He favoured one leg, injured on the Night of Eshsen. He was wearing torn pyjamas, mud-stained and rain-sodden. His greying hair hung in lank festoons around his ears and over his forehead. Twice the height of his captors, he held himself very stiff, and stared at them in courageous, angry misery. "What you want?"

"We must talk, Mr Gosse," said Selver, who had learned plain English from Lyubov. "I'm Selver of the Ash Tree of Eshreth. I'm Lyubov's friend."

"Yes, I know you. What have you to say?"

"I have to say that the killing is over, if that be made a promise kept by your people and my people. You may all go free, if you will gather in your people from the logging camps in South Sornol, Kushil, and Rieshwel, and make them all stay together here. You may live here where the forest is dead, where you grow your seed-grasses. There must not be any more cutting of trees."

Gosse's face had grown eager: "The camps weren't attacked?"

"No."

Gosse said nothing.

Selver watched his face, and presently spoke again: "There are less than two thousand of your people left living in the world, I think. Your women are all dead. In the other camps there are still weapons; you could kill many of us. But we have some of your weapons. And there are more of us than you could kill. I suppose you know that, and that's why you have not tried to have the flying ships bring you fire-throwers, and kill the guards, and escape. It would be no good; there really are so many of us. If you make the promise with us it will be much the best, and then you can wait without harm until one of your Great Ships comes, and you can leave the world. That will be in three years, I think."

"Yes, three local years— How do you know that?"

"Well, slaves have ears, Mr Gosse."

Gosse looked straight at him at last. He looked away, fidgeted, tried to ease his leg. He looked back at Selver, and away again. "We had already 'promised' not to hurt any of your people. It's why the workers were sent home. It did no good, you didn't listen—"

"It was not a promise made to us."

"How can we make any sort of agreement or treaty with a people who have no government, no central authority?"

"I don't know. I'm not sure you know what a promise is. This one was soon broken."

"What do you mean? By whom, how?"

"In Rieshwel, New Java. Fourteen days ago. A town was burned and its people killed by yumens of the Camp in Rieshwel."

"What are you talking about?"

"About news brought us by messengers from Rieshwel."

"It's a lie. We were in radio contact with New Java right along, until the massacre. Nobody was killing natives there or anywhere else."

"You're speaking the truth you know," Selver said, "I the truth I know. I accept your ignorance of the killings on Rieshwel; but you must accept my telling you that they were done. This remains: the promise must be made to us and with us, and it must be kept. You'll wish to talk about these matters with Colonel Dongh and the others."

Gosse moved as if to re-enter the gate, then turned back and said in his deep, hoarse voice, "Who are you, Selver? Did you—was it you that organised the attack? Did you lead them?"

"Yes, I did."

"Then all this blood is on your head," Gosse said, and with sudden savagery, "Lyubov's too, you know. He's dead—your 'friend Lyubov'."

Selver did not understand the idiom. He had learned murder, but of guilt he knew little beyond the name. As his gaze locked for a moment with Gosse's pale, resentful stare, he felt afraid. A sickness rose up in him, a mortal chill. He tried to put it away from him, shutting his eyes a moment. At last he said, "Lyubov is my friend, and so not dead."

"You're children," Gosse said with hatred. "Children, savages. You have no conception of reality. This is no dream, this is real! You killed Lyubov. He's dead. You killed the women—the *women*—you burned them alive, slaughtered them like animals!"

"Should we have let them live?" said Selver with vehemence equal to Gosse's, but softly, his voice singing a little. "To breed like insects in the carcase of the World? To overrun us? We killed them to sterilise you. I know what a realist is, Mr Gosse, Lyubov and I have talked about these words. A realist is a man who knows both the world and his own dreams. You're not sane: there's not one man in a thousand of you who knows how to dream. Not even Lyubov and he was the best among you. You sleep, you wake and forget your dreams, you sleep again and wake again, and so you spend your whole lives, and you think that is being, life, reality! You are not children, you are grown men, but insane. And that's why we had to kill you, before you drove us mad. Now go back and talk about reality with the other insane men. Talk long, and well!"

The guards opened the gate, threatening the crowding yumens inside with their spears; Gosse re-entered the compound, his big shoulders hunched as if against the rain.

Selver was very tired. The headwoman of Berre and another woman came to him and walked with him, his arms over their shoulders so that if he stumbled he should not fall. The young hunter Greda, a cousin of his Tree, joked with him, and Selver answered light-headedly, laughing. The walk back to Endtor seemed to go on for days.

He was too weary to eat. He drank a little hot broth and lay down by the Men's Fire. Endtor was no town but a mere camp by the great river, a favourite fishing place for all the cities that had once been in the forest round about, before the yumens came. There was no Lodge. Two fire-rings of black stone and a long grassy bank over the river where tents of hide and plaited rush could be set up, that was Endtor. The river Menend, the master river of Sornol, spoke ceaselessly in the world and in the dream at Endtor.

There were many old men at the fire, some whom he knew from Broter and Tuntar and his own destroyed city Eshreth, some whom he did not know; he could see in their eyes and gestures, and hear in their voices, that they were Great Dreamers; more dreamers than had ever been gathered in one place before, perhaps. Lying stretched out full length, his head raised on his hands, gazing at the fire, he said, "I have called the yumens mad. Am I mad myself?"

"You don't know one time from the other," said old Tubab, laying a pine-knot on the fire, "because you did not dream either sleeping or waking for far too long. The price for that takes long to pay."

"The poisons the yumens take do much the same as does the lack of sleep and dream," said Heben, who had been a slave both at Central and at Smith Camp. "The yumens poison themselves in order to dream. I saw the dreamer's look in them after they took the poisons. But they couldn't call the dreams, nor control them, nor weave nor shape nor cease to dream; they were driven, overpowered. They did not know what was within them at all. So it is with a man who hasn't dreamed for many days. Though he be the wisest of his Lodge, still he'll be mad, now and then, here and there, for a long time after. He'll be driven, enslaved. He will not understand himself."

A very old man with the accent of South Sornol laid his hand on Selver's shoulder, caressing him, and said, "My dear young god, you need to sing, that would do you good."

"I can't. Sing for me."

The old man sang; others joined in, their voices high and reedy, almost tuneless, like the wind blowing in the water-reeds of Endtor. They sang one of the songs of the ash-tree, about the delicate parted leaves that turn yellow in autumn when the berries turn red, and one night the first frost silvers them.

While Selver was listening to the song of the Ash, Lyubov lay down beside him. Lying down he did not seem so monstrously tall and large-limbed. Behind him was the half-collapsed, fire-gutted building, black against the stars. "I am like you," he said, not looking at Selver, in that dream-voice which tries to reveal its own untruth. Selver's heart was heavy with sorrow for his friend. "I've got a headache," Lyubov said in his own voice, rubbing the back of his neck as he always did, and at that Selver reached out to touch him, to console him. But he was shadow and firelight in the world-time, and the old men were singing the song of the

Ash, about the small white flowers on the black branches in spring among the parted leaves.

The next day the yumens imprisoned in the compound sent for Selver. He came to Eshsen in the afternoon, and met with them outside the compound, under the branches of an oak tree, for all Selver's people felt a little uneasy under the bare open sky. Eshsen had been an oak grove; this tree was the largest of the few the colonists had left standing. It was on the long slope behind Lyubov's bungalow, one of the six or eight houses that had come through the night of the burning undamaged. With Selver under the oak were Reswan, the headwoman of Berre, Greda of Cadast, and others who wished to be in on the parley, a dozen or so in all. Many bowmen kept guard, fearing the yumens might have hidden weapons, but they sat behind bushes or bits of wreckage left from the burning, so as not to dominate the scene with the hint of threat. With Gosse and Colonel Dongh were three of the yumens called officers and two from the logging camp, at the sight of one of whom, Benton, the ex-slaves drew in their breaths. Benton had used to punish "lazy creechies" by castrating them in public.

The Colonel looked thin, his normally yellow-brown skin a muddy yellow-grey; his illness had been no sham. "Now the first thing is," he said when they were all settled, the yumens standing, Selver's people squatting or sitting on the damp, soft oak-leaf mould, "the first thing is that I want first to have a working definition of just precisely what these terms of yours mean and what they mean in terms of guaranteed safety of my personnel under my command here."

There was a silence.

"You understand English, don't you, some of you?"

"Yes. I don't understand your question, Mr Dongh."

"Colonel Dongh, if you please!"

"Then you'll call me Colonel Selver, if you please." A singing note came into Selver's voice; he stood up, ready for the contest, tunes running in his mind like rivers.

But the old yumen just stood there, huge and heavy,

angry yet not meeting the challenge. "I did not come here
to be insulted by you little humanoids," he said. But his lips
trembled as he said it. He was old, and bewildered, and
humiliated. All anticipation of triumph went out of Selver.
There was no triumph in the world any more, only death.
He sat down again. "I didn't intend insult, Colonel Dongh,"
he said resignedly. "Will you repeat your question, please?"

"I want to hear your terms, and then you'll hear ours, that's
all there is to it."

Selver repeated what he had said to Gosse.

Dongh listened with apparent impatience. "All right. Now
you don't realise that we've had a functioning radio in the
prison compound for three days now." Selver did know this,
as Reswan had at once checked on the object dropped by the
helicopter, lest it be a weapon; the guards reported it was a
radio, and he let the yumens keep it. Selver merely nodded.
"So we've been in contact with the three outlying camps, the
two on King Land and one on New Java, right along, and
if we had decided to make a break for it and escape from that
prison compound then it would have been very simple for us
to do that, with the helicopters to drop us weapons and covering our movements with their mounted weapons, one flame-
thrower could have got us out of the compound and in case
of need they also have the bombs that can blow up an entire
area. You haven't seen those in action of course."

"If you'd left the compound, where would you have gone?"

"The point is, without introducing into this any beside
the point or erroneous factors, now we are certainly greatly
outnumbered by your forces, but we have the four helicopters at the camps, which there's no use you trying to
disable as they are under fully armed guard at all times now,
and also all the serious fire-power, so that the cold reality
of the situation is we can pretty much call it a draw and
speak in positions of mutual equality. This of course is a
temporary situation. If necessary we are enabled to maintain
a defensive police action to prevent all-out war. Moreover
we have behind us the entire fire-power of the Terran Inter-

stellar Fleet, which could blow your entire planet right out
of the sky. But these ideas are pretty intangible to you, so
let's just put it as plainly and simply as I can, that we're
prepared to negotiate with you, for the present time, in terms
of an equal frame of reference."

Selver's patience was short; he knew his ill-temper was a
symptom of his deteriorated mental state, but he could no
longer control it. "Go on, then!"

"Well, first I want it clearly understood that as soon as we
got the radio we told the men at the other camps not to
bring us weapons and not to try any airlift or rescue attempts,
and reprisals were strictly out of order—"

"That was prudent. What next?"

Colonel Dongh began an angry retort, then stopped; he
turned very pale. "Isn't there anything to sit down on," he
said.

Selver went around the yumen group, up the slope, into the
empty two room bungalow, and took the folding desk-chair.
Before he left the silent room he leaned down and laid his
cheek on the scarred, raw wood of the desk, where Lyubov
had always sat when he worked with Selver or alone; some
of his papers were lying there now; Selver touched them
lightly. He carried the chair out and set it in the rainwet dirt
for Dongh. The old man sat down, biting his lips, his almond-
shaped eyes narrow with pain.

"Mr Gosse, perhaps you can speak for the Colonel,"
Selver said. "He isn't well."

"I'll do the talking," Benton said, stepping forward, but
Dongh shook his head and muttered, "Gosse."

With the Colonel as auditor rather than speaker it went
more easily. The yumens were accepting Selver's terms. With
a mutual promise of peace, they would withdraw all their
outposts and live in one area, the region they had forested
in Middle Sornol: about 1700 square miles of rolling land,
well watered. They undertook not to enter the forest; the
forest people undertook not to trespass on the Cut Lands.

The four remaining airships were the cause of some argument. The yumens insisted they needed them to bring their people from the other islands to Sornol. Since the machines carried only four men and would take several hours for each trip, it appeared to Selver that the yumens could get to Eshsen rather sooner by walking, and he offered them ferry service across the straits; but it appeared that yumens never walked far. Very well, they could keep the hoppers for what they called the "Airlift Operation". After that, they were to destroy them— Refusal. Anger. They were more protective of their machines than of their bodies. Selver gave in, saying they could keep the hoppers if they flew them only over the Cut Lands and if the weapons in them were destroyed. Over this they argued, but with one another, while Selver waited, occasionally repeating the terms of his demand, for he was not giving in on this point.

"What's the difference, Benton," the old Colonel said at last, furious and shaky, "can't you see that we can't use the damned weapons? There's three million of these aliens all scattered out all over every damned island, all covered with trees and undergrowth, no cities, no vital network, no centralised control. You can't disable a guerrilla type structure with bombs, it's been proved, in fact my own part of the world where I was born proved it for about thirty years fighting off major super-powers one after the other in the twentieth century. And we're not in a position until a ship comes to prove our superiority. Let the big stuff go, if we can hold on to the side-arms for hunting and self-defence!"

He was their Old Man, and his opinion prevailed in the end, as it might have done in a Men's Lodge. Benton sulked. Gosse started to talk about what would happen if the truce was broken, but Selver stopped him. "These are possibilities, we aren't yet done with certainties. Your Great Ship is to return in three years, that is three and a half years of your count. Until that time you are free here. It will not be very hard for you. Nothing more will be taken away from Centralville, except some of Lyubov's work that I wish to keep. You still have most of your tools of tree-cutting and ground-moving; if you need more tools, the iron-mines of Peldel are in your territory. I think all this is clear. What remains to be known is this: When that ship comes, what will they seek to do with you, and with us?"

"We don't know," Gosse said. Dongh amplified: "If you hadn't destroyed the ansible communicator first thing off, we might be receiving some current information on these matters, and our reports would of course influence the decisions that may be made concerning a finalised decision on the status of this planet, which we might then expect to begin to implement before the ship returns from Prestno. But due to wanton destruction due to your ignorance of your own interests, we haven't even got a radio left that will transmit over a few hundred miles."

"What is the ansible?" The word had come up before in this talk; it was a new one to Selver.

"ICD," the Colonel said, morose.

"A kind of radio," Gosse said, arrogant. "It put us in instant touch with our home-world."

"Without the 27-year waiting?"

Gosse stared down at Selver. "Right. Quite right. You learned a great deal from Lyubov, didn't you?"

"Didn't he just," said Benton. "He was Lyubov's little green buddyboy. He picked up everything worth knowing and a bit more besides. Like all the vital points to sabotage, and where the guards would be posted, and how to get into the weapon stockpile. They must have been in touch right up to the moment the massacre started."

Gosse looked uneasy. "Raj is dead. All that's irrelevant now, Benton. We've got to establish—"

"Are you trying to infer in some way that Captain Lyubov was involved in some activity that could be called treachery to the Colony, Benton?" said Dongh, glaring and pressing his hands against his belly. "There were no spies or treachers on my staff, it was absolutely handpicked before we ever left Terra and I know the kind of men I have to deal with."

"I'm not inferring anything, Colonel. I'm saying straight out that it was Lyubov stirred up the creechies, and if orders hadn't been changed on us after that Fleet ship was here, it would never have happened."

Gosse and Dongh both started to speak at once. "You are all very ill," Selver observed, getting up and dusting himself off, for the damp brown oak-leaves clung to his short body-fur as to silk. "I'm sorry we've had to hold you in the creechie-pen, it is not a good place for the mind. Please send for your men from the camps. When all are here and the large weapons have been destroyed, and the promise has been spoken by all of us, then we shall leave you alone. The gates of the compound will be opened when I leave here today. Is there more to be said?"

None of them said anything. They looked down at him. Seven big men, with tan or brown hairless skin, cloth-covered, dark-eyed, grim-faced; twelve small men, green or brownish-green, fur-covered, with the large eyes of the semi-nocturnal creature, with dreamy faces; between the two groups, Selver, the translator, frail, disfigured, holding all their destinies in his empty hands. Rain fell softly on the brown earth about them.

"Farewell then," Selver said, and led his people away.

"They're not so stupid," said the headwoman of Berre as she accompanied Selver back to Endtor. "I thought such giants must be stupid, but they saw that you're a god, I saw it in their faces at the end of the talking. How well you talk that gobble-gubble. Ugly they are, do you think even their children are hairless?"

"That we shall never know, I hope."

"Ugh, think of nursing a child that wasn't furry. Like trying to suckle a fish."

"They are all insane," said old Tubab, looking deeply distressed. "Lyubov wasn't like that, when he used to come to Tuntar. He was ignorant, but sensible. But these ones, they argue, and sneer at the old man, and hate each other, like this," and he contorted his grey-furred face to imitate the expressions of the Terrans, whose words of course he had not been able to follow. "Was that what you said to them, Selver, that they're mad?"

"I told them that they were ill. But then, they've been defeated, and hurt, and locked in that stone cage. After that anyone might be ill and need healing."

"Who's to heal them," said the headwoman of Berre, "their women are all dead. Too bad for them. Poor ugly things—great naked spiders they are, ugh!"

"They are men, men, like us, men," Selver said, his voice shrill and edged like a knife.

"Oh, my dear lord god, I know it, I only meant they *look* like spiders," said the old woman, caressing his cheek. "Look here, you people, Selver is worn out with this going back and forth between Endtor and Eshsen, let's sit down and rest a bit."

"Not here," Selver said. They were still in the Cut Lands, among stumps and grassy slopes, under the bare sky. "When we come under the trees...." He stumbled, and those who were not gods helped him to walk along the road.

CHAPTER SEVEN

Davidson found a good use for Major Muhamed's tape re-
corder. Somebody had to make a record of events on New
Tahiti, a history of the crucifixion of the Terran Colony. So
that when the ships came from Mother Earth they could
learn the truth. So that future generations could learn how
much treachery and cowardice and folly humans were cap-
able of, and how much courage against all odds. During his
free moments—not much more than moments since he had
assumed command—he recorded the whole story of the
Smith Camp Massacre, and brought the record up to date
for New Java, and for King and Central also, as well as he
could with the garbled hysterical stuff that was all he got
by way of news from Central HQ.

Exactly what had happened there nobody would ever
know, except the creechies, for the humans were trying to
cover up their own betrayals and mistakes. The outlines were
clear, though. An organised bunch of creechies, led by
Selver, had been let into the Arsenal and the Hangars, and
turned loose with dynamite, grenades, guns, and flamethrowers to totally destruct the city and slaughter the humans.
It was an inside job, the fact that HQ was the first place
blown up proved that. Lyubov of course had been in on it,
and his little green buddies had proved just as grateful as
you might expect, and cut his throat like the others. At
least, Gosse and Benton claimed to have seen him dead the
morning after the massacre. But could you believe any of
them, actually? You could assume that any human left alive
in Central after that night was more or less of a traitor. A
traitor to his race.

The women were all dead, they claimed. That was bad enough, but what was worse, there was no reason to believe it. It was easy for the creechies to take prisoners in the woods, and nothing would be easier to catch than a terrified girl running out of a burning town. And wouldn't the little green devils like to get hold of a human girl and try experiments on her? God knows how many of the women were still alive in the creechie warrens, tied down underground in one of those stinking holes, being touched and felt and crawled over and defiled by the filthy, hairy little monkeymen. It was unthinkable. But by God sometimes you have to be able to think about the unthinkable.

A hopper from King had dropped the prisoners at Central a receiver-transmitter the day after the massacre, and Muhamed had taped all his exchanges with Central starting that day. The most incredible one was a conversation between him and Colonel Dongh. The first time he played it Davidson had torn the thing right off the reel and burned it. Now he wished he had kept it, for the records, as a perfect proof of the total incompetence of the C.O.'s at both Central and New Java. He had given in to his own hotbloodedness, destroying it. But how could he sit there and listen to the recording of the Colonel and the Major discussing total surrender to the creechies, agreeing not to try retaliation, not to defend themselves, to give up all their big weapons, to all squeeze together onto a bit of land picked out for them by the creechies, a reservation conceded to them by their generous conquerors, the little green beasts. It was incredible. Literally incredible.

Probably old Ding Dong and Moo were not actually traitors by intent. They had just gone spla, lost their nerve. It was this damned planet that did it to them. It took a very strong personality to withstand it. There was something in the air, maybe pollens from all those trees, acting as some kind of drug maybe, that made ordinary humans begin to get as stupid and out of touch with reality as the creechies were. Then, being so outnumbered, they were pushovers for the creechies to wipe out.

It was too bad Muhamed had had to be put out of the way, but he would never have agreed to accept Davidson's plans, that was clear; he'd been too far gone. Anyone who'd heard that incredible tape would agree. So it was better he got shot before he really knew what was going on, and now no shame would attach to his name, as it would to Dongh's and all the other officers left alive at Central.

Dongh hadn't come on the radio lately. Usually it was Juju Sereng, in Engineering. Davidson had used to pal around a lot with Juju and had thought of him as a friend, but now you couldn't trust anybody any more. And Juju was another asiatiform. It was really queer how many of them had survived the Centralville Massacre; of those he'd talked to, the only non-asio was Gosse. Here in Java the fifty-five loyal men remaining after the reorganisation were mostly eurafs like himself, some afros and afrasians, not one pure asio. Blood tells, after all. You couldn't be fully human without some blood in your veins from the Cradle of Man. But that wouldn't stop him from saving those poor yellow bastards at Central, it just helped explain their moral collapse under stress.

"Can't you realise what kind of trouble you're making for us, Don?" Juju Sereng had demanded in his flat voice. "We've made a formal truce with the creechies. And we're under direct orders from Earth not to interfere with the hilfs and not to retaliate. Anyhow how the hell can we retaliate? Now all the fellows from King Land and South Central are here with us we're still less than two thousand, and what have you got there on Java, about sixty-five men isn't it? Do you really think two thousand men can take on three million intelligent enemies, Don?"

"Juju, fifty men can do it. It's a matter of will, skill, and weaponry."

"Batshit! But the point is, Don, a truce has been made. And if it's broken, we've had it. It's all that keeps us afloat, now.

Maybe when the ship gets back from Prestno and sees what happened, they'll decide to wipe out the creechies. We don't know. But it does look like the creechies intend to keep the truce, after all it was their idea, and we have got to. They can wipe us out by sheer numbers, any time, the way they did Centralville. There were thousands of them. Can't you understand that, Don?"

"Listen, Juju, sure I understand. If you're scared to use the three hoppers you've still got there, you could send 'em over here, with a few fellows who see things like we do here. If I'm going to liberate you fellows singlehanded, I sure could use some more hoppers for the job."

"You aren't going to liberate us, you're going to incinerate us, you damned fool. Get that last hopper over here to Central now: that's the Colonel's personal order to you as Acting C.O. Use it to fly your men here; twelve trips, you won't need more than four local dayperiods. Now act on those orders, and get to it." Ponk, off the air—afraid to argue with him any more.

At first he worried that they might send their three hoppers over and actually bomb or strafe New Java Camp; for he was, technically, disobeying orders, and old Dongh wasn't tolerant of independent elements. Look how he'd taken it out on Davidson already, for that tiny reprisal-raid on Smith. Initiative got punished. What Ding Dong liked was submission, like most officers. The danger with that is that it can make the officer get submissive himself. Davidson finally realised, with a real shock, that the hoppers were no threat to him, because Dongh, Sereng, Gosse, even Benton were *afraid* to send them. The creechies had ordered them to keep the hoppers inside the Human Reservation: and they were obeying orders.

Christ, it made him sick. It was time to act. They'd been waiting around nearly two weeks now. He had his camp well defended; they had strengthened the stockade fence and built it up so that no little green monkeymen could possibly get over it, and that clever kid Aabi had made lots of neat home-made land mines and sown 'em all around the stockade in a hundred-metre belt. Now it was time to show the creechies that they might push around those sheep on Central but on New Java it was men they had to deal with. He took the hopper up and with it guided an infantry squad of fifteen to a creechie-warren south of camp. He'd learned how to spot the things from the air; the giveaway was the orchards, concentrations of certain kinds of tree, though not planted in rows like humans would. It was incredible how many warrens there were once you learned to spot them. The forest was crawling with the things. The raiding party burned up that warren by hand, and then flying back with a couple of his boys he spotted another, less than four kilos from camp. On that one, just to write his signature real clear and plain for everybody to read, he dropped a bomb. Just a firebomb, not a big one, but baby did it make the green fur fly. It left a big hole in the forest, and the edges of the hole were burning.

Of course that was his real weapon when it actually came to setting up massive retaliation. Forest fire. He could set one of these whole islands on fire, with bombs and firejelly dropped from the hopper. Have to wait a month or two, till the rainy season was over. Should he burn King or Smith or Central? King first, maybe, as a little warning, since there were no humans left there. Then Central, if they didn't get in line.

"What are you trying to do?" said the voice on the radio, and it made him grin, it was so agonised, like some old woman being held up. "Do you know what you're doing, Davidson?"

"Yep."

"Do you think you're going to subdue the creechies?" It wasn't Juju this time, it might be that bigdome Gosse, or any of them; no difference; they all bleated baa.

"Yes, that's right," he said with ironic mildness.

"You think if you keep burning up villages they'll come to you and surrender—three million of them. Right?"

"Maybe."

"Look, Davidson," the radio said after a while, whining and buzzing; they were using some kind of emergency rig, having lost the big transmitter, along with that phoney ansible which was no loss. "Look, is there somebody else standing by there we can talk to?"

"No; they're all pretty busy. Say, we're doing great here, but we're out of dessert stuff, you know, fruit cocktail, peaches, crap like that. Some of the fellows really miss it. And we were due for a load of maryjanes when you fellows got blown up. If I sent the hopper over, could you spare us a few crates of sweet stuff and grass?"

A pause. "Yes, send it on over."

"Great. Have the stuff in a net, and the boys can hook it without landing." He grinned.

There was some fussing around at the Central end, and all of a sudden old Dongh was on, the first time he'd talked to Davidson. He sounded feeble and out of breath on the whining shortwave. "Listen, Captain, I want to know if you fully realise what form of action your actions on New Java are going to be forcing me into taking. If you continue to disobey your orders. I am trying to reason with you as a reasonable and loyal soldier. In order to ensure the safety of my personnel here at Central I'm going to be put into the position of being forced to tell the natives here that we can't assume any responsibility at all for your actions."

"That's correct, sir."

"What I'm trying to make clear to you is that means that we are going to be put into the position of having to tell them that we can't stop you from breaking the truce there on Java. Your personnel there is sixty-six men, is that correct, well I want those men safe and sound here at Central with us to wait for the *Shackleton* and keep the Colony together. You're on a suicide course and I'm responsible for those men you have there with you."

"No, you're not, sir. I am. You just relax. Only when you see the jungle burning, pick up and get out into the middle of a Strip, because we don't want to roast you folks along with the creechies."

"Now listen, Davidson, I order you to hand your command over to Lt. Temba at once and report to me here," said the distant whining voice, and Davidson suddenly cut off the radio, sickened. They were all spla, playing at still being soldiers, in full retreat from reality. There were actually very few men who could face reality when the going got tough.

As he expected, the local creechies did absolutely nothing about his raids on the warrens. The only way to handle them, as he'd known from the start, was to terrorise them and never let up on them. If you did that, they knew who was boss, and knuckled under. A lot of the villages within a thirty-kilo radius seemed to be deserted now before he got to them, but he kept his men going out to burn them up every few days.

The fellows were getting rather jumpy. He had kept them logging, since that's what forty-eight of the fifty-five loyal survivors were, loggers. But they knew that the robo-freighters from Earth wouldn't be called down to load up the lumber, but would just keep coming in and circling in orbit waiting for the signal that didn't come. No use cutting trees just for the hell of it; it was hard work. Might as well burn them. He exercised the men in teams, developing fire-setting techniques. It was still too rainy for them to do much, but it kept their minds busy. If only he had the other three hoppers, he'd really be able to hit and run. He considered a raid on Central to liberate the hoppers, but did not yet mention this idea even to Aabi and Temba, his best men. Some of the boys would get cold feet at the idea of an armed raid on their own HQ. They kept talking about "when we get back with the others". They didn't know those others had abandoned them, betrayed them, sold their skins to the creechies. He didn't tell them that, they couldn't take it.

One day he and Aabi and Temba and another good sound man would just take the hopper over, then three of them jump out with machine guns, take a hopper apiece, and so home again, home again, jiggety jog. With four nice egg-beaters to beat eggs with. Can't make an omelette without beating eggs. Davidson laughed aloud, in the darkness of his bungalow. He kept that plan hidden just a little longer, because it tickled him so much to think about it.

After two more weeks they had pretty well closed out the creechie-warrens within walking distance, and the forest was neat and tidy. No vermin. No smoke-puffs over the trees. Nobody hopping out of bushes and flopping down on the ground with their eyes shut, waiting for you to stomp them. No little green men. Just a mess of trees and some burned places. The boys were getting really edgy and mean; it was time to make the hopper-raid. He told his plan one night to Aabi, Temba, and Post.

None of them said anything for a minute, then Aabi said, "What about fuel, Captain?"

"We got enough fuel."

"Not for four hoppers; wouldn't last a week."

"You mean there's only a month's supply left for this one?"

Aabi nodded.

"Well then, we pick up a little fuel too, looks like."

"How?"

"Put your minds to it."

They all sat there looking stupid. It annoyed him. They looked to him for everything. He was a natural leader, but he liked men who thought for themselves too. "Figure it out, it's your line of work, Aabi," he said, and went out for a smoke, sick of the way everybody acted, like they'd lost their nerve. They just couldn't face the cold hard facts.

They were low on maryjanes now and he hadn't had one for a couple of days. It didn't do anything for him. The night was overcast and black, damp, warm, smelling like spring. Ngenene went by walking like an ice-skater, or almost like a robot on treads; he turned slowly through a gliding step and gazed at Davidson, who stood on the bungalow porch in the dim light from the doorway. He was a power-saw operator, a huge man. "The source of my energy is connected to the

Great Generator I cannot be switched off," he said in a level tone, gazing at Davidson.

"Get to your barracks and sleep it off!'" Davidson said in the whipcrack voice that nobody ever disobeyed, and after a moment Ngenene skated carefully on, ponderous and graceful. Too many of the men were using hallies more and more heavily. There was plenty, but the stuff was for loggers relaxing on Sundays, not for soldiers of a tiny outpost marooned on a hostile world. They had no time for getting high, for dreaming. He'd have to lock the stuff up. Then some of the boys might crack. Well, let 'em crack. Can't make an omelette without cracking eggs. Maybe he could send them back to Central in exchange for some fuel. You give me two, three tanks of gas and I'll give you two, three warm bodies, loyal soldiers, good loggers, just your type, a little far gone in bye-bye dreamland....

He grinned, and was going back inside to try this one out on Temba and the others, when the guard posted up on the lumberyard smoke stack yelled. "They're coming!" he screeched out in a high voice, like a kid playing Blacks and Rhodesians. Somebody else over on the west side of the stockade began yelling too. A gun went off.

And they came. Christ, they came. It was incredible. There were thousands of them, thousands. No sound, no noise at all, until that screech from the guard; then one gunshot; then an explosion—a land mine going up—and another, one after another, and hundreds and hundreds of torches flaring up lit one from another and being thrown and soaring through the black wet air like rockets, and the walls of the stockade coming alive with creechies, pouring in, pouring over, pushing, swarming, thousands of them. It was like an army of rats Davidson had seen once when he was a little kid, in the last Famine, in the streets of Cleveland, Ohio, where he grew up. Something had driven the rats out of their holes and they had come up in daylight, seething up over the wall, a pulsing blanket of fur and eyes and little hands and teeth, and he had yelled for his mom and run like crazy, or was that only a dream he'd had when he was a kid? It was important to keep cool. The hopper was parked in the creechie-pen; it was still dark over on that side and he got there at once. The gate was locked, he always kept it locked in case one of the weak sisters got a notion of flying off to Papa Ding Dong some dark night. It seemed to take a long time to get the key out and fit it in the lock and turn it right, but it was just a matter of keeping cool, and then it took a long time to sprint to the hopper and unlock it. Post and Aabi were with him now. At last came the huge rattle of the rotors, beating eggs, covering up all the weird noises, the high voices yelling and screeching and singing. Up they went, and hell dropped away below them: a pen full of rats, burning.

"It takes a cool head to size up an emergency situation quickly," Davidson said. "You men thought fast and acted fast. Good work. Where's Temba?"

"Got a spear in his belly," Post said.

Aabi, the pilot, seemed to want to fly the hopper, so Davidson let him. He clambered into one of the rear seats and sat back, letting his muscles relax. The forest flowed beneath them, black under black.

"Where you heading, Aabi?"

"Central."

"No. We don't want to go to Central."

"Where do we want to go to?" Aabi said with a kind of womanish giggle. "New York? Peking?"

"Just keep her up a while, Aabi, and circle camp. Big circles. Out of earshot."

"Captain, there isn't any Java Camp any more by now," said Post, a logging-crew foreman, a stocky, steady man.

"When the creechies are through burning the camp, we'll come in and burn creechies. There must be four thousand of them all in one place there. There's six flamethrowers in the back of this helicopter. Let's give 'em about twenty minutes. Start with the jelly bombs and then catch the ones that run with the flamethrowers."

"Christ," Aabi said violently, "some of our guys might be there, the creechies might take prisoners, we don't know. I'm not going back there and burn up humans, maybe." He had not turned the hopper.

Davidson put the nose of his revolver against the back of Aabi's skull and said, "Yes, we're going back; so pull yourself together, baby, and don't give me a lot of trouble."

"There's enough fuel in the tank to get us to Central, Captain," the pilot said. He kept trying to duck his head away from the touch of the gun, like it was a fly bothering him. "But that's all. That's all we got."

"Then we'll get a lot of mileage out of it. Turn her, Aabi."

"I think we better go on to Central, Captain," Post said in his stolid voice, and this ganging up against him enraged Davidson so much that reversing the gun in his hand he struck out fast as a snake and clipped Post over the ear with the gun-butt. The logger just folded over like a Christmas card, and sat there in the front seat with his head between his knees and his hands hanging to the floor. "Turn her, Aabi," Davidson said, the whiplash in his voice. The helicopter swung around in a wide arc. "Hell, where's camp, I never had this hopper up at night without any signal to follow," Aabi said, sounding dull and snuffly like he had a cold.

"Go east and look for the fire," Davidson said, cold and quiet. None of them had any real stamina, not even Temba. None of them had stood by him when the going got really tough. Sooner or later they all joined up against him, because they just couldn't take it the way he could. The weak conspire against the strong, the strong man has to stand alone and look out for himself. It just happened to be the way things are. Where was the camp?

They should have been able to see the burning buildings for miles in this blank dark, even in the rain. Nothing showed. Grey-black sky, black ground. The fires must have gone out. Been put out. Could the humans have driven off the creechies? After he'd escaped? The thought went like a spray of icewater through his mind. No, of course not, not fifty against thousands. But by God there must be a lot of pieces of blown-up creechie lying around on the minefields, anyway. It was just that they'd come so damned thick. Nothing could have stopped them. He couldn't have planned for that. Where had they come from? There hadn't been any creechies in the forest anywhere around for days and days. They must have poured in from somewhere, from all directions, sneaking along in the woods, coming up out of their holes like rats. There wasn't any way to stop thousands and thousands of them like that. Where the hell was camp? Aabi was tricking, faking course. "Find the camp, Aabi," he said softly.

"For Christ's sake I'm trying to," the boy said.

Post never moved, folded over there by the pilot.

"It couldn't just disappear, could it, Aabi. You got seven minutes to find it."

"Find it yourself," Aabi said, shrill and sullen.

"Not till you and Post get in line, baby. Take her down lower."

After a minute Aabi said, "That looks like the river."

There was a river, and a big clearing; but where was Java Camp? It didn't show up as they flew north over the clearing. "This must be it, there isn't any other big clearing is there," Aabi said, coming back over the treeless area. Their landing-lights glared but you couldn't see anything outside the tunnels of the lights; it would be better to have them off. Davidson reached over the pilot's shoulder and switched the lights off. Blank wet dark was like black towels slapped on their eyes. "For Christ's sake!" Aabi screamed, and flipping the lights back on slewed the hopper left and up, but not fast enough. Trees leaned hugely out of the night and caught the machine.

The vanes screamed, hurling leaves and twigs in a cyclone through the bright lanes of the lights, but the boles of the trees were very old and strong. The little winged machine plunged, seemed to lurch and tear itself free, and went down sideways into the trees. The lights went out. The noise stopped.

"I don't feel so good," Davidson said. He said it again. Then he stopped saying it for there was nobody to say it to. Then he realised he hadn't said it anyway. He felt groggy. Must have hit his head. Aabi wasn't there. Where was he? This was the hopper. It was all slewed around, but he was still in his seat. It was so dark, like being blind. He felt around, and so found Post, inert, still doubled up, crammed in between the front seat and the control panel. The hopper trembled whenever Davidson moved, and he figured out at last that it wasn't on the ground but wedged in between trees, stuck like a kite. His head was feeling better, and he wanted more and more to get out of the black, tilted-over cabin. He squirmed over into the pilot's seat and got his legs out, hung by his hands, and could not feel ground, only branches scraping his dangling legs. Finally he let go, not knowing how far he'd fall, but he had to get out of that cabin. It was only a few feet down. It jolted his head, but he felt better standing up. If only it wasn't so dark, so black. He had a torch in his belt, he always carried one at night around camp. But it wasn't there. That was funny. It must have fallen out. He'd better get back into the hopper and get it. Maybe Aabi had taken it. Aabi had intentionally crashed the hopper, taken Davidson's torch, and made a break for it. The slimy little bastard, he was like all the rest of them. The air was black and full of moisture, and you couldn't tell where to put your feet, it was all roots and bushes and tangles. There were noises all around, water dripping, rustling, tiny noises, little things sneaking around in the darkness. He'd better get back up into the hopper, get his torch. But he couldn't see how to climb back up. The bottom edge of the doorway was just out of reach of his fingers.

There was a light, a faint gleam seen and gone away off in the trees. Aabi had taken the torch and gone off to reconnoitre, get orientated, smart boy. "Aabi!" he called in a piercing whisper. He stepped on something queer while he was trying to see the light among the trees again. He kicked at it with his boots, then put a hand down on it, cautiously, for it wasn't wise to go feeling things you couldn't see. A lot of wet stuff, slick, like a dead rat. He withdrew his hand quickly. He felt in another place after a while; it was a boot under his hand, he could feel the crossings of the laces. It must be Aabi lying there right under his feet. He'd got thrown out of the hopper when it came down. Well, he'd deserved it with his Judas trick, trying to run off to Central. Davidson did not like the wet feel of the unseen clothes and hair. He straightened up. There was the light again, black-barred by near and distant tree-trunks, a distant glow that moved.

Davidson put his hand to his holster. The revolver was not in it.

He'd had it in his hand, in case Post or Aabi acted up. It was not in his hand. It must be up in the helicopter with his torch.

He stood crouching, immobile; then abruptly began to run. He could not see where he was going. Tree-trunks jolted him from side to side as he knocked into them, and roots tripped up his feet. He fell full length, crashing down among bushes. Getting to hands and knees he tried to hide. Bare, wet twigs dragged and scraped over his face. He squirmed farther into the bushes. His brain was entirely occupied by the complex smells of rot and growth, dead leaves, decay, new shoots, fronds, flowers, the smells of night and spring and rain. The light shone full on him. He saw the creechies.

He remembered what they did when cornered, and what Lyubov had said about it. He turned over on his back and lay with his head tipped back, his eyes shut. His heart stuttered in his chest.

Nothing happened.

It was hard to open his eyes, but finally he managed to. They just stood there: a lot of them, ten or twenty. They carried those spears they had for hunting, little toy-looking things but the iron blades were sharp, they could cut right through your guts. He shut his eyes and just kept lying there.

And nothing happened.

His heart quieted down, and it seemed like he could think better. Something stirred down inside him, something almost like laughter. By God they couldn't get him down! If his own men betrayed him, and human intelligence couldn't do any more for him, then he used their own trick against them—played dead like this, and triggered this instinct reflex that kept them from killing anybody who took that position. They just stood around him, muttering at each other. *They couldn't hurt him.* It was as if he was a god.

"Davidson."

He had to open his eyes again. The resin-flare carried by one of the creechies still burned, but it had grown pale, and the forest was dim grey now, not pitch-black. How had that happened? Only five or ten minutes had gone by. It was still hard to see but it wasn't night any more. He could see the leaves and branches, the forest. He could see the face looking down at him. It had no colour in this toneless twilight of dawn. The scarred features looked like a man's. The eyes were dark holes.

"Let me get up," Davidson said suddenly in a loud, hoarse voice. He was shaking with cold from lying on the wet ground. He could not lie there with Selver looking down at him.

Selver was emptyhanded, but a lot of the little devils around him had not only spears but revolvers. Stolen from his stockpile at camp. He struggled to his feet. His clothes clung icy to his shoulders and the backs of his legs, and he could not stop shaking.

"Get it over with," he said. "Hurry-up-quick!"

Selver just looked at him. At least now he had to look up, way up, to meet Davidson's eyes.

"Do you wish me to kill you now?" he inquired. He had learned that way of talking from Lyubov, of course; even his voice, it could have been Lyubov talking. It was uncanny.

"It's my choice, is it?"

"Well, you have lain all night in the way that means you wished us to let you live; now do you want to die?"

The pain in his head and stomach, and his hatred for this horrible little freak that talked like Lyubov and that had got him at its mercy, the pain and the hatred combined and set his belly churning, so he retched and was nearly sick. He shook with cold and nausea. He tried to hold on to courage. He suddenly stepped forward a pace and spat in Selver's face.

There was a little pause, and then Selver, with a kind of dancing movement, spat back. And laughed. And made no move to kill Davidson. Davidson wiped the cold spittle off his lips.

"Look, Captain Davidson," the creechie said in that quiet little voice that made Davidson go dizzy and sick, "we're both gods, you and I. You're an insane one, and I'm not sure whether I'm sane or not. But we are gods. There will never be another meeting in the forest like this meeting now between us. We bring each other such gifts as gods bring. You gave me a gift, the killing of one's kind, murder. Now, as well as I can, I give you my people's gift, which is not killing. I think we each find each other's gift heavy to carry. However, you must carry it alone. Your people at Eshsen tell me that if I bring you there, they have to make a judgment on you and kill you, it's their law to do so. So, wishing to give you life, I can't take you with the other prisoners to Eshsen; and I can't leave you to wander in the forest, for you do too much harm. So you'll be treated like one of us when we go mad. You'll be taken to Rendlep where nobody lives any more, and left there."

Davidson stared at the creechie, could not take his eyes off it. It was as if it had some hypnotic power over him. He couldn't stand this. Nobody had any power over him. Nobody could hurt him. "I should have broken your neck right away, that day you tried to jump me," he said, his voice still hoarse and thick.

"It might have been best," Selver answered. "But Lyubov prevented you. As he now prevents me from killing you—

All the killing is done now. And the cutting of trees. There aren't trees to cut on Rendlep. That's the place you call Dump Island. Your people left no trees there, so you can't make a boat and sail from it. Nothing much grows there any more, so we shall have to bring you food and wood to burn. There's nothing to kill on Rendlep. No trees, no people. There were trees and people, but now there are only the dreams of them. It seems to me a fitting place for you to live, since you must live. You might learn how to dream there, but more likely you will follow your madness through to its proper end, at last."

"Kill me now and quit your damned gloating."

"Kill you?" Selver said, and his eyes looking up at Davidson seemed to shine, very clear and terrible, in the twilight of the forest. "I can't kill you, Davidson. You're a god. You must do it yourself."

He turned and walked away, light and quick, vanishing among the grey trees within a few steps.

A noose slipped over Davidson's head and tightened a little on his throat. Small spears approached his back and sides. They did not try to hurt him. He could run away, make a break for it, they didn't dare kill him. The blades were polished, leaf-shaped, sharp as razors. The noose tugged gently at his neck. He followed where they led him.

CHAPTER EIGHT

Selver had not seen Lyubov for a long time. That dream had gone with him to Rieshwel. It had been with him when he spoke the last time to Davidson. Then it had gone, and perhaps it slept now in the grave of Lyubov's death at Eshsen, for it never came to Selver in the town of Broter where he now lived.

But when the great ship returned, and he went to Eshsen, Lyubov met him there. He was silent and tenuous, very sad, so that the old carking grief awoke in Selver.

Lyubov stayed with him, a shadow in the mind, even when he met the yumens from the ship. These were people of power; they were very different from all yumens he had known, except his friend, but they were much stronger men than Lyubov had been.

His yumen speech had gone rusty, and at first he mostly let them talk. When he was fairly certain what kind of people they were, he brought forward the heavy box he had carried from Broter. "Inside this there is Lyubov's work, " he said, groping for the words. "He knew more about us than the others do. He learned my language and the Men's Tongue; we wrote all that down. He understood somewhat how we live and dream. The others do not. I'll give you the work, if you'll take it to the place he wished."

The tall, white-skinned one, Lepennon, looked happy, and thanked Selver, telling him that the papers would indeed be taken where Lyubov wished, and would be highly valued. That pleased Selver. But it had been painful to him to speak his friend's name aloud, for Lyubov's face was still bitterly sad when he turned to it in his mind. He withdrew a little from the yumens, and watched them. Dongh and Gosse and others of Eshsen were there along with the five from the ship. The new ones looked clean and polished as new iron. The old ones had let the hair grow on their faces, so that they looked a little like huge, black-furred Athsheans. They still wore clothes, but the clothes were old and not kept clean. They were not thin, except for the Old Man, who had been ill ever since the Night of Eshsen; but they all looked a little like men who are lost or mad.

This meeting was at the edge of the forest, in that zone where by tacit agreement neither the forest people nor the yumens had built dwellings or camped for these past years. Selver and his companions settled down in the shade of a big ash-tree that stood out away from the forest eaves. Its berries were only small green knots against the twigs as yet, its leaves were long and soft, labile, summer-green. The light beneath the great tree was soft, complex with shadows.

The yumens consulted and came and went, and at last one came over to the ash-tree. It was the hard one from the ship, the Commander. He squatted down on his heels near Selver, not asking permission but not with any evident intention of rudeness. He said, "Can we talk a little?"

"Certainly."

"You know that we'll be taking all the Terrans away with us. We brought a second ship with us to carry them. Your world will no longer be used as a colony."

"This was the message I heard at Broter, when you came three days ago."

"I wanted to be sure that you understand that this is a permanent arrangement. We're not coming back. Your world has been placed under the League Ban. What that means in your terms is this: I can promise you that no one will come here to cut the trees or take your lands, so long as the League lasts."

"None of you will ever come back," Selver said, statement or question.

"Not for five generations. None. Then perhaps a few men,

ten or twenty, no more than twenty, might come to talk to
your people, and study your world, as some of the men here
were doing."

"The scientists, the Speshes," Selver said. He brooded. "You
decide matters all at once, your people," he said, again between statement and question.

"How do you mean?" The Commander looked wary.

"Well, you say that none of you shall cut the trees of
Athshe: and all of you stop. And yet you live in many
places. Now if a headwoman in Karach gave an order, it would
not be obeyed by the people of the next village, and surely not
by all the people in the world at once...."

"No, because you haven't one government over all. But
we do—now—and I assure you its orders are obeyed. By all of
us at once. But, as a matter of fact, it seems to me from the
story we've been told by the colonists here, that when *you*
gave an order, Selver, it was obeyed by everybody on every
island here at once. How did you manage that?"

"At that time I was a god," Selver said, expressionless.

After the Commander had left him, the long white one
came sauntering over and asked if he might sit down in
the shade of the tree. He had tact, this one, and was extremely
clever. Selver was uneasy with him. Like Lyubov, this one
would be gentle; he would understand, and yet would himself be utterly beyond understanding. For the kindest of them
was as far out of touch, as unreachable, as the cruellest. That
was why the presence of Lyubov in his mind remained
painful to him, while the dreams in which he saw and touched
his dead wife Thele were precious and full of peace.

"When I was here before," Lepennon said, "I met this man,
Raj Lyubov. I had very little chance to speak with him,
but I remember what he said; and I've had time to read some
of his studies of your people, since. His work, as you say. It's
largely because of that work of his that Athshe is now free
of the Terran Colony. This freedom had become the direction
of Lyubov's life, I think. You, being his friend, will see that

his death did not stop him from arriving at his goal, from finishing his journey."

Selver sat still. Uneasiness turned to fear in his mind. This one spoke like a Great Dreamer.

He made no response at all.

"Will you tell me one thing, Selver. If the question doesn't offend you. There will be no more questions after it. . . . There were the killings: at Smith Camp, then at this place, Eshsen, then finally at New Java Camp where Davidson led the rebel group. That was all. No more since then. . . . Is that true? Have there been no more killings?"

"I did not kill Davidson."

"That does not matter," Lepennon said, misunderstanding; Selver meant that Davidson was not dead, but Lepennon took him to mean that someone else had killed Davidson. Relieved to see that the yumen could err, Selver did not correct him.

"There has been no more killing, then?"

"None. They will tell you," Selver said, nodding towards the Colonel and Gosse.

"Among your own people, I mean. Athsheans killing Athsheans."

Selver was silent.

He looked up at Lepennon, at the strange face, white as the mask of the Ash Spirit, that changed as it met his gaze.

"Sometimes a god comes," Selver said. "He brings a new way to do a thing, or a new thing to be done. A new kind of singing, or a new kind of death. He brings this across the bridge between the dream-time and the world-time. When he has done this, it is done. You cannot take things that exist in the world and try to drive them back into the dream, to hold them inside the dream with walls and pretences. That is insanity. What is, is. There is no use pretending, now, that we do not know how to kill one another."

Lepennon laid his long hand on Selver's hand, so quickly and gently that Selver accepted the touch as if the hand were not a stranger's. The green-gold shadows of the ash leaves flickered over them.

"But you must not pretend to have reasons to kill one another. Murder has no reason," Lepennon said, his face as anxious and sad as Lyubov's face. "We shall go. Within two days we shall be gone. All of us. Forever. Then the forests of Athshe will be as they were before."

Lyubov came out of the shadows of Selver's mind and said, "I shall be here."

"Lyubov will be here," Selver said. "And Davidson will be here. Both of them. Maybe after I die people will be as they were before I was born, and before you came. But I do not think they will."

Ursula K. Le Guin was born in 1929 into an academic household – her father was an eminent anthropologist while her mother was a writer. She herself obtained a Masters degree in Romance Literature following her undergraduate degree. Her first story was published in *Fantastic* magazine in 1962, and her first novel was *Rocannon's World* (1966), set in her Hainish universe. Her fourth novel, *The Left Hand of Darkness* (1969), was critically acclaimed and won both the Hugo and Nebula Awards for Best Novel. She repeated this feat with *The Dispossessed* (1974). The Earthsea series, which began with *A Wizard of Earthsea* (1968), has also attained undisputed classic status. Her recent series, the Annals of the Western Shore, has won her the PEN Center USA Children's literature award and the Nebula Award for best novel. In 2014 Ursula Le Guin was awarded the National Book Foundation Medal for Distinguished Contribution to American Letters. She passed away in 2018.

A full list of SF Masterworks can be found at
www.gollancz.co.uk

THE of BOOKS EARTHSEA

Now for the first time ever, all together in one volume, comes *The Books of Earthsea*. This contains the early short stories, Le Guin's 'Earthsea Revisioned' Oxford lecture, and new Earthsea stories, never before printed. With a new introduction by Le Guin herself, this essential edition also includes over fifty illustrations by renowned artist Charles Vess, specially commissioned and selected by Le Guin, to bring her refined vision of Earthsea and its people to life in a totally new way.

ABOUT GOLLANCZ

Gollancz is the oldest SF publishing imprint in the world. Since being founded in 1927 Gollancz has continued to publish a focused selection of bestselling and award-winning authors. The front-list includes **Ben Aaronovitch**, **Joe Abercrombie**, **Charlaine Harris**, **Joanne Harris**, **Joe Hill**, **Alastair Reynolds**, **Patrick Rothfuss**, **Nalini Singh** and **Brandon Sanderson**.

As one of the largest Science Fiction and Fantasy imprints in the UK it is no surprise we have one of the most extensive backlists in the world. Find high-quality SF on Gateway written by such authors as **Philip K. Dick**, **Ursula Le Guin**, **Connie Willis**, **Sir Arthur C. Clarke**, **Pat Cadigan**, **Michael Moorcock** and **George R.R. Martin**.

We also have a strand of publishing in translation, which includes French, Polish and Russian authors. Gollancz is home to more award-winning authors than any other imprint, with names including **Aliette de Bodard**, **M. John Harrison**, **Paul McAuley**, **Sarah Pinborough**, **Pierre Pevel**, **Justina Robson** and many more.

The SF Gateway
More than 3,000 classic, rare and previously out-of-print SF novels at your fingertips.
www.sfgateway.com

The Gollancz Blog
Bringing you news from our worlds to yours. Stories, interviews, articles and exclusive extracts just for you!
www.gollancz.co.uk

GOLLANCZ
LONDON